Florence Marryat

The Prey of the Gods

Vol. II

Florence Marryat

The Prey of the Gods
Vol. II

ISBN/EAN: 9783337052201

Printed in Europe, USA, Canada, Australia, Japan

Cover: Foto ©Andreas Hilbeck / pixelio.de

More available books at **www.hansebooks.com**

THE PREY OF THE GODS.

A Novel.

BY FLORENCE MARRYAT,

(MRS. ROSS CHURCH)

AUTHOR OF "LOVE'S CONFLICT," "VERONIQUE," "HER LORD
AND MASTER," ETC., ETC.

" Where, when the Gods would be cruel,
Do they go for a torture ?—where
Plant thorns, set pain like a jewel ?
Ah ! not in the flesh, not there !
The rocks of the earth, and the rods
Are weak as foam on the sands ;
In the heart is the prey of the Gods,
Who crucify hearts—not hands."
A. C. SWINBURNE.

" If the sense is hard
To alien ears, I did not speak to these.
No, not to thee, but to thyself in me."—TENNYSON.

IN THREE VOLUMES.

VOL. II.

LONDON:

RICHARD BENTLEY AND SON,

NEW BURLINGTON STREET.

1871.

CONTENTS OF VOL. II.

CHAPTER		PAGE
I.	SAVED FROM HERSELF	1
II.	A MESSAGE FROM HEAVEN	17
III.	THE PRESENTIMENT FULFILLED	52
IV.	A FRESH ALARM	71
V.	UNEXPECTED VISITORS	95
VI.	UNEXPECTED NEWS	123
VII.	THE FALLEN IDOL	147
VIII.	HIS FRIENDS' OPINIONS	162
IX.	THE BRIDEGROOM ELECT.	182
X.	A GREAT CHANGE	196
XI.	WIDOWHOOD	225
XII.	THE ORCHARD HOUSE	241
XIII.	RUN TO EARTH	262

THE PREY OF THE GODS.

CHAPTER I.

SAVED FROM HERSELF.

WITH a vague notion that once alone she will be enabled to recover the shock which her own words have brought upon her, Lady Gwynne flies to the shelter of her sleeping chamber, and enters it with haste, but her footsteps are arrested on the very threshold.

For there before her, straight in her path, as the Angel stood to confront Balaam in his career of disobedience, stands the little table which holds her manuals of devotion, with the sacred crucifix suspended on the wall above it. How often has she knelt before that table, blistering the pages of her prayer-book with her tears, as she lamented the frailty and weakness of her disposition, and made fierce resolutions to do better for the future. How has she kept those holy resolutions ? amended that pitiable defection ?

She stands for one moment rooted to the spot that has been the altar of so many hopes and fears, gazing with a wild, nameless terror at the image of the Sacred Body, to all appearance hanging so helplessly from the tree of death, and yet with the mighty power to save a world, even by the recollection that brings with it one sigh of faithful regret ; and then, scared by the remembrance of herself, and of her promise, Lady Gwynne rushes away again, and slams the door behind her.

Down-stairs,—not to the shrubbery,— not to the presence of him whom she has thenceforth constituted her protector and adviser, but out by the carriage drive, and into the silent, green fields, where she can be alone and think.

There, with flushed cheeks, excited mien, and wild, bright eyes, she paces to and fro, walking at the rate of about six miles an hour, and quite unconscious of the extraordinary appearance her behaviour must assume to those who may see it from the high road, whilst she ponders on the fate she has carved out for herself.

She thinks of the morrow : of the hour

she has appointed in which to meet her lover; that fatal hour, already so near at hand, which will for ever separate her from her home,—her station in society,—her child,—the company of all modest women and right-minded men.

She tries to imagine what it must feel like, to have lost all claim to be considered virtuous: to know one's name is bandied about in public, and the details of one's weakness made the subject for a leading article in every penny newspaper: to be pointed out as a *divorcée*, and become a pariah and outcast from all companionship but that of women who have fallen like herself.

Fallen !—pshaw ! 'Tis the mere cant of the world : the name that men have chosen as a deterrent to the act ! How can she fall lower than she has already done ? What degradation waits her greater than the name of wife to Lyster Gwynne? She does not believe in it; such bug-bears have no power to frighten her!

On one side she sees love and liberty; on the other, abhorrence and despair! No alternative presents itself to her fevered imagination.

She pictures the fair life that she will lead with Auberon Slade: the scenes of beauty in which they will linger: the endless vista of peace that stretches out before them: the loving dependance with which they will lean on one another!

And then he will rise! build up his fame, as he scarcely dares to hope that he will build it now, and she shall be ever by his side to cheer him on; to bear a humble hand in all his labours; and to exult in his success. And when she sees him, by virtue of his talent, moving in a higher sphere than that to which he has been born ; bowed down to by the great and noble, and flattered by his fellow-labourers ; how gladly will she retire in the background, and be content to know, without hearing it, that she reaps by right a portion of his triumph.

But will he so rise ? be so received ? As the doubt springs into birth, a pang shoots through her heart. Oh, if, instead of helping, she should be the one to drag him down ! For herself, Lady Gwynne cares nothing. Scorn, contumely and reproach would not have the power to provoke a sigh from her, if their sting were made harmless by her lover's smile, or their bitterness assuaged by his honied words of comfort !

But without that antidote, if he too should feel them, not for her, but for himself, what joy could life hold for her? She recalls the refinement of his mind, his extra-sensitiveness about trifles, the little courage or perseverance he displays in overcoming the difficulties in his path (she might, too, had she recognised it, have recalled the selfishness displayed even in his love for her!), and shudders at the thought. Was it, could it be possible, that at some future day Auberon Slade might be tempted, by ill luck or want of success, to turn round upon herself, and make the frightful doubt that has flashed through her mind, a certainty?

Oh, no! Impossible! Guilty and despicable in the world's eyes as she will soon become, God is more pitiful than men, and will command death to approach her in

some more merciful guise than in such words
from *him!* But here is the gilt stripped
off the ginger-bread indeed; and as Lady
Gwynne contemplates the mere possibility
of so terrible a requital for her projected
sacrifice, she stops short in her rapid pacing
to and fro, and, sinking down upon the
herbage of the rich solitary pasture land
which she is traversing, hides her hot
cheeks in the long cool grass, and gives free
vent to the current of her sad thoughts.
Oh, is there no possible alternative to a
career of shame? no other means of escape
from the net in which their feet have become so hopelessly entangled? no way by
which she can save Auberon Slade from
the horrors of remorse, and herself the risk
of some day hearing from his lips that she
has been the destroyer of both his earthly
and his heavenly prospects? no manner in

which she may yet send him from her, contented, if not happy?

She presses her grief-stained face upon the grass, and tries to solve the problem; but it is too hard for her.

She sees herself, left desolate in Felton Hall, her only solace wandering about the paths which they have trod together, pursuing her avocations without interest, her duties without zest, and growing thinner and paler, and more hopeless, until death mercifully releases her from all her sufferings.

And then, she pictures him, sorrowing and alone, bereft (as he himself had said) of hope and her at the same moment; without an aim in life; sinking lower and lower in the world's repute; until he comes to curse the disappointment that helped to keep him down.

She could endure to contemplate the other fiction, for she is strong and lion-hearted, as the sequel will depict her, and able to bear any amount of pain that only affects herself—but this one is too much.

Auberon! who has never loved another woman as he loves her; who would live but half a life without her presence; was it possible that she could rob him of what he had rightly called his due, break her pledged word, take back her gift at the eleventh hour?

No! it is not to be thought of. She is no longer her own; she has given herself away. It is for him to decide upon her future fate.

Should he love her and care for her to the very end, she will be the happiest woman on the face of the earth. Should he tire of her (oh, pray ! pray Heaven, that he never may !), she can but creep away from him and die (as she must die if she renounces him) in solitude and misery !

And she is so proud, 'midst all her humiliation and her shame, to think that she has a reputation and a name to sacrifice for him who has become all the world to her.

She meditates so deeply that she does not hear a step approach her through the rich thick grass, and when Mr. Lawrence's voice strikes on her ear, she starts from her recumbent posture, as though she had been detected in a crime.

" My dear Lady Gwynne ! this is hardly prudent. The afternoons begin to close in so early now, and we had a shower last night !"

She rises immediately, and with considerable confusion proffers him her hand.

She holds her head down as she does so ; but Mr. Lawrence notes her crimsoned cheeks, and strange disordered air.

"Can you find no fitter place for quiet thought, dear friend, than these damp fields ?"

"Oh, yes ! of course ; but it is so cool and pleasant here. How did you see me ?"

"I was walking along the path on the other side of the hedge, and happening to glance over, I caught sight of your figure. I was afraid at first that something must have happened. You have given me quite a fright."

"I am so sorry. It is evident you are not used to see me in my fits of sulks. You have been to the Hall ?"

"No. I have just come from administering the sacrament to a dying man at the other end of the village. It was a most beautiful and impressive sight. I wish you had been with me."

She does not answer him, nor does she make the least attempt to progress in either direction. She only stands where she has risen, playing with the numerous trifles attached to her watch-chain, and keeping her eyes carefully fixed upon the ground.

"You are coming to church, I presume?" says Mr. Lawrence; "shall we walk there together?"

"No, not to-day, I think," she stammers —"that is to say——"

"It is Friday," he answers gently, "and I should like to see you in your place this afternoon."

But still she hesitates, and is evidently distressed.

"Have you any engagement to detain you, Lady Gwynne?"

Deceit is not one of her failings, and she blunders out the truth before she knows it.

"Oh, no! I am quite at leisure, only—"

"Only what?"

"I feel so awfully miserable and unsettled this afternoon, Mr. Lawrence, and church is sure to upset me,"—and he sees the tears dropping slowly on her ungloved hands.

"If that is the case, there is all the more reason you should seek comfort where it is alone to be found, Lady Gwynne, and decision, where it is alone to be depended upon."

She moves a little way towards him then, but her lips breathe no consent to his proposal.

"Come! you have often let me decide for you in greater matters than this. Take my advice now, and accompany me to evensong. I am sure you will feel the better for it."

"Oh, no! oh, no! indeed," shrinking

backwards, "you cannot tell—if you knew as I know myself, you would not ask it!"

"There is but One can do that," he rejoins gravely, "but I know, Lady Gwynne, that whatever trouble you may be labouring under, whether it be an affliction of your own making; of the tyranny of man, or the dispensation of God; I cannot do wrong in inviting you to seek ease and comfort, and a settled mind before the altar, or in thinking you will not permit so old, and I may add, so sincere a friend, to ask you in vain."

She looks up in the kind face bent so earnestly upon her; she remembers that she may never so look upon it again; that this may be the last time he will ever ask a favour of her; and her good angel takes her by the hand, and propels her footsteps in the same direction as the vicar's.

He smiles as he observes the action, but he makes no comment on it; and side by side, they tread the path that leads to where the bell is sounding cheerfully for evensong.

CHAPTER II.

A MESSAGE FROM HEAVEN.

SIDE by side, yet not together; in company, but alone; they walk silent and abstracted, each heart occupied with its own sad thoughts; and his, perhaps, the sadder of the two. For Mr. Lawrence has been watching over this poor soul with jealous anxiety for weeks past, and, but a few days since, thought that he observed symptoms that his fears regarding it were false.

And how thankfully he would have acknowledged he had been wrong; have

called himself suspicious, illiberal, and un-
generous; anything, in fact, sooner than have
received such a confirmation of the dreaded
truth, that Lady Gwynne has something
very serious preying on her mind, as seems
to be conveyed to him by the attitude of
despair in which he has detected her, this
afternoon.   For he is well acquainted with
her character and disposition, and knows she
is not one of those fiery and undisciplined
natures, who care little what the world
thinks of them, so long as they indulge their
feelings by a vulgar and boisterous exhibition of grief.   He has seen her suffering
for years; putting up in silence and patience
with petty indignities, slight neglects,
and covert sneers that would have turned
many another woman, naturally sweet-tem-
pered as herself, into little less than a domestic fiend; and he has admired her for-

bearance, and prayed for her relief. And he feels that if Gwendoline Gwynne can cast herself down upon the ground, and bury her tears in the grass, like any impetuous unbridled girl, who has been disappointed in her first love, there must be something of very serious import oppressing her mind; some vivid danger threatening her safety. And as they come in sight of the church, whose portals stand wide open to invite all those who are weary and heavy laden to enter there, and leave their cares behind, a sudden conviction comes over Mr. Lawrence, that the golden opportunities are flying; that there is a stringent necessity for making an immediate appeal to this woman's conscience, and that much of the welfare of her future life depends upon the spirit in which she shall leave God's house that day. Which causes him, whilst in the sacristy, to offer up a prayer that something may occur in the evening service to touch her heart in the right manner, and bring her to those Feet that have never yet been known to spurn the contrite soul; and with the same hope and intention running through his mind, he astonishes the choir by suddenly changing the simple hymn that has been fixed for the day, to one, which ordinarily they never sing except in Lent.

Meanwhile Lady Gwynne creeps into her seat, and sits down there, almost sullenly.

She has been entrapped into going to church, but she has no inclination to pray or sing; for her heart is in a state of semi-rebellion against the Almighty for having made her life miserable, and encompassed her with temptation, and permitted things to go so far, that she has no alternative but to fly in His face, and outrage His commandments. She believes, or she attempts to believe, that He is hard upon her; that He has tried her strength too much, and caused her to pass through a fiery ordeal that not the best of men, even His own servants of old, had been found brave enough to resist.

And how can she, a poor, weak, persecuted woman, be expected to triumph, where they failed? It is absurd, unreasonable, impossible; and if what she is about to do will shut her out from heaven, it will be heaven's fault, not hers.

And yet above all the perverse reasoning of her disobedient and rebellious soul, she is conscious of a continual rapping at her heart—a rapping which she would deaden, if she could, but cannot; the knock as of One who waits outside, but will come in and sup, so soon as she shall open the door to Him.

Oh! open it, Gwendoline! throw wide the portals, lest the messenger grow weary and depart, never again to beckon you to heaven with that patient gracious Hand!

The evening services commence; they are simple and unmeretricious, and not particularly calculated to melt a stubborn spirit into tears; yet, as they proceed, something in them—perhaps it is merely the resonance of the old familiar words; perhaps, the thought that by that time to-morrow she will have forfeited all right to worship with her fellow Christians—touches the heart of Lady Gwynne, and her head sinks lower and lower, and tears find their way even through the clasped fingers that hide her conscious-stricken face.

Oh! is it possible she is about to give up all this; to make *him* give it up; that they shall never be able to kneel together in the sanctuary and ask God's blessing on their ways, and words, and acts?

How should they?

The very horror with which she shrinks from the idea, proves the insult they are about to offer to the Majesty on High :—

> "Weary of earth and laden with my sin,
> I look at Heaven and long to enter in;
> But there no evil thing may find a home,
> And yet I hear a voice that bids me 'Come!'"

The fresh young voices of the choir have commenced to chant the hymn that Mr. Lawrence chose for them; but though she knows that they are singing, she hardly notes the words, so absorbed is she in the fearful question that has presented itself to her mind.

No more prayers! How shall she pray for a broken and a contrite heart whilst living in a state of hardened sin; or for a

blessing upon him who shares her guilt ; or
for a peaceful death that can but introduce
her to that lot, reserved for all who die
impenitent ?

And then the Blessed Sacrament ! Oh,
agony ! to think she never more may approach, nor feed upon the Bread of Everlasting Life !—

> " So vile I am, how dare I hope to stand
> In the pure glory of that holy land ?
> Before the whiteness of that Throne appear ?
> Yet there are hands stretched out to draw me near."

How foolish she is to think of it ! These
are, of course, some of the things that she
must—that she has promised to give up for
Auberon's sake ! He must be her religion,
her prayers, her everything thenceforth !

She has chosen her fate ; it is already
irrevocable. She can only make matters
worse by looking back.

> " The while I fain would tread the heavenly way,
>   Evil is present with me, day by day :
>   Yet on mine ears, the gracious tidings fall,
>   Repent ! Confess ! thou shalt be loosed from all."

Oh ! how hot and uncomfortable she has become ; there must surely be a thunderstorm brewing in the air.   The windows of the church are all set open, yet Lady Gwynne feels as though she could hardly bear the weight of her straw hat and summer mantle, and pushes the damp hair impatiently from her forehead.   Yes ! she once had wished—she had even tried to tread the heavenly way ! her conscience can attest so far ; but circumstances have been all against her.   She is too weak to struggle alone, and she has had no helper.

Oh, if her poor mother had but lived ! Can her parents be looking down upon her now ?

> " It is the voice of JESUS that I hear ;
>   His are the hands stretched out to draw me near,
>   And His the blood that can for all atone,
>   And set me faultless there before His Throne."

Is it—can it be possible—that It ever will atone for such a fault as she is about to commit? Oh! the ignominy, the outrage, the bitter, bitter shame that she will bring on all who love her, or with whom she is connected :—on Auberon, and Daisy, and herself—and perhaps on others, yet to come! The blackness of the crime to which she has consented, in revenge against her hus-band, and the life that Heaven designed for her, seems in her fevered mind to stretch out, through endless generations, and to involve creature after creature in its conse-quences, until it culminates before the Judgment Seat of God; and terror stricken by the picture her imagination has conjured up, Lady Gwynne sinks upon her knees, and with her face buried in her hands, remains dead to everything except the fearful beating of her heart, and the wish that she might quit at once a world in which she is no longer fit to live.

So she remains until the service is concluded; and then the sudden lulling of the choristers' chanting, and the sound of Mr. Lawrence's grave voice as he pronounces the final benediction, once more rouse her to a sense of where she is.

But she will not rise; she is ashamed to show her tear-stained countenance to the villagers, who will, one and all, comment on the reason of her grief; and the little congregation file out slowly from the sacred building, and she is still upon her knees.

Then the altar is covered up; the doors are gently closed; and, thinking she is at last alone, Lady Gwynne gives full vent to her distress. She has pent it up for several hours; she has fought against conviction, and tried to smile away her scruples, but that gentle Hand is still tapping on the portals of her heart, and she can fight and smile no longer.

The baseness of her ingratitude, the hardihood of her contempt, the outrage she would cast upon His Mercy, are all vividly portrayed to her; and, penitent—abashed—remorseful—as though her sin had been already sinned, she answers the invitation of that pierced Hand, and throwing wide the door, falls prostrate in an agony of grief.

Her sobs resound throughout the empty building, yet, had it been full of hearers, it would have made no difference to her then, for she is conscious but of one thing—that she is alone with her own heart and Him!

But after a little while, the lapse of a few minutes only, a footstep pauses before the crouching form of the awakened woman, and a voice sounds in her ear,—"Do not stay here, my child ! Come into the sacristy, I want to speak to you !"

She had not expected to see or hear him more, and she guesses intuitively what he is about to say to her ; and yet she rises, almost with eagerness, and turning on him eyes that are half blinded with what they have gone through, places her hot trembling hand in his, and ejaculates, in a solemn whisper,—"Oh ! save me, for God's sake !"

He makes no answer, except by leading her up the aisle, and into the small bare room containing only a deal table and a couple of chairs, which he calls his sacristy, and having entered which, he closes the door carefully behind them. And then he places her in a seat, for her limbs are failing, and she scarcely seems capable of finding one for herself; and taking a chair opposite, waits patiently until she shall see fit to unburden her mind to him.

But Lady Gwynne only casts herself across the table, in an attitude of the deepest despair, and five—ten minutes have elapsed, and yet she still continues to sob upon her outstretched arms.

"Well, my child! and from what am I to save you?" demanded the kind fatherly voice at last.

"From myself," she answers hoarsely.

"And in what way?" But to this question there is no reply.

"This is no time nor place for reserve between us," says Mr. Lawrence presently; "and I know you will forgive an old friend, like myself, for telling you that I have long observed your weakness and distress, and feared that it might lead to evil consequences."

" Ah ! you cannot tell how evil."

" I ean guess, my child ! Do you imagine that because it is my duty to point out the path that leads to perfection to my fellow men, I must therefore have forgotten what it is to sin myself ? I wish to God I had."

She glances up into the calm face that is regarding her with looks of such intense compassion ; she marks the serious glance, the humble reverence, the holy sympathy ; and feeling as though an angel had been sent from Heaven to direct her in the right way, springs from her seat with a sudden cry, and casts herself upon the ground before him.

" No ! no ! dear Lady Gwynne ! not there !"

" Yes ! yes ! here ; where else should I be, but at the feet I am not worthy to embrace? Oh! save me! save me from myself. You think you know—but you can never, *never* guess, how wicked I have been."

"But you repent!"

"No—no!—I cannot repent; there is no repentance in me. If you rescue me, you must do it by force, and you must do it to-day—to-morrow will be too late!"

"*To-morrow!*" He almost staggers back beneath the thought.

"Yes—I am on the point of committing an awful crime. Oh! if you could but save me."

"You shall be saved," he answers, solemnly, "though not by me. There hangs your Deliverer, and the Deliverer of the whole world," pointing to the crucifix which forms the solitary ornament of the bare room that holds them.

"I dare not look at It," she murmurs, with a shudder.

"But you must—you shall look at It. Look at It, as the poisoned Israelites gazed at the brazen serpent; cling to It, as the drowning man clings to the spar that is his only chance of safety; embrace It, as the sick and polluted embraced the garments of their Lord. I cannot help you else."

"I dare not! I have cut myself off from It, and all Its promises for evermore. Hope is over for me—I am not worthy—I have gone too far!"

"And yet you ask me to rescue you," he says, with a look of reproach.

"Oh! I was wrong—it is useless; I have passed my promise, and I cannot retract! If I thought that you would permit the name of such a wretch as I am, to pass your lips in prayer, I might ask you sometimes, after to-morrow, to pray for me, and —and—*all I love*—but it would pollute them—you must not think of it."

He tries to raise her, fearing her agitation should be too much for her strength; but she resists him, and, as he reseats himself, she is still grovelling at his feet.

"To pray for you, and for all whom you love," he repeats solemnly. "Yes! you have my promise, and, whatever happens, you may count upon my doing that, until the last day of your life, or mine. There *are* some, then, Lady Gwynne, whom you love—for whom, perhaps, you think that you are willing to sacrifice your happiness— even to lay down your life !"

"Oh! yes! indeed I am. Oh, Mr. Lawrence, if you only knew—if I could make you understand *how much* I love him, you would pity more than you would blame me !"

She has given him the loophole he desired, and he can say what he likes to her now.

" I can quite imagine it, my child. You love him so devotedly, so truly, so un-selfishly, that you have no hesitation in risking his eternal salvation !"

" Ah !" she says, in the same tone in which she would have said it, had a sharp knife been run into her side.

" In casting shame and obloquy upon his earthly career ; in cutting him off from all the sweet, and ennobling effects of domestic life ; in dragging him downwards on the path of sin ; and of finally consigning his precious and immortal soul, for the salva-tion of which the death of a God was not thought too great a sacrifice, to everlasting damnation."

" Oh, spare me—spare me !"

But it is not his object to tone, or soften down, the glaring colours in which he desires to depict her future to her.

" I do not speak of your own shame; of your deserted child ; your forsaken duties ; of the numbers that will be involved in the pain of your disgrace ; because I know that to a distorted imagination and disordered mind, such crimes will but appear to enhance the sacrifice love calls on you to make ; but I tell you, Lady Gwynne (and I stand here this moment as the messenger of God to you), that, if after the solemn warning He sends you by my lips to-day, you persevere in attempting to wrest from His Hands the soul for which He died, you will act a part worthy of the foul Fiend himself, and for which you will be but fitly rewarded if that soul rises up hereafter in hell to reproach you with its eternal loss."

" Oh, what *shall* I do ? what *shall* I do ?"

" And putting aside the awful risk I have presented to you, what excuse could you find for so requiting the heavenly love, the fatherly care that has pervaded your whole life ?   What earthly creature has loved you as your Lord has loved you ? what care has so preserved you ? what tenderness enveloped your existence ?   To whom can you owe so large a debt of gratitude, so great a sacrifice, so inexhaustible a fund of thanks ?   Who else has borne with you, suffered with you, bled for you, as He has ?"

" Oh, Mr. Lawrence ! tell me in God's name, what shall I do ?"

At the tone of submission in which these words are uttered, all the sternness dies out of his voice, and his next sentence is one of unutterable sweetness.

"There is but one thing for you to do, my child. To take in your hand this love, this intention, this desire, of which, however sinful, God knows the value in your eyes; and give it to Him, Who gave up all for you."

"Will He accept it?"

"Accept it? It will be the sweetest offering you have ever laid upon His altar, for it is your all. Don't think I underrate the sacrifice, or the obedience. I know the anguish it will cause you; but if it costs your life, it will not be too great a gift to give to Him."

She rises without aid, and stands by the table, steadily and alone; but Mr. Lawrence is almost frightened at the change that has taken place in her countenance. It looks as pale, and as fixed, as though in death.

"*I will do it!*"

She only says these four words; but there is a world of determination, and an eternity of pain conveyed by the voice in which she says them; and Mr. Lawrence feels the tears well up into his own eyes.

"God help you, my daughter;" and for a little space there is silence between them.

"I know," says Lady Gwynne presently, but she speaks very slowly, "that you are right. I have known it all along. I know also that it is the kindest thing that I can do for him. But—but—it will kill me!"

He does not attempt to soothe her; he knows it is not the time.

"Even so! It is happier to die, doing the will of God, than to live, the slave of Satan."

"He will never forgive me. He will think I do not love him," she whispers despairingly.

"If he blames you here, he will bless you hereafter!"

"But—but—he will be so lonely. No! don't look like that—I mean indeed—I mean to do what is right; only let me gain a little more strength, a little more courage, and to-morrow I will tell him all."

The priest's face clouds over.

"Lady Gwynne, to-morrow may be too late; God calls you to obey *to-day*. Sin is the cancer of the soul, and if you desire to live, you must cut it out at once; you must neither spare nor cry, but plunge the knife in to the very heft, and root out the deadly evil. Come, you are braver and stronger than most women, and will succeed where others would faint or fail. Let me see you call all your strength and courage to your aid, and regarding this sore temptation as a means by which you may prove your love to God, surmount it as a Christian should."

" Ah, you think so much too highly of me. For myself, I might be able to do all this ; but you do not know what a pitiful coward I become, when the knife has to be used on him. Oh, Mr. Lawrence!" she cries, casting herself again upon her knees before him, whilst a tempest of grief shakes her frail being to its core, " pray, pray, bless me ! or I shall never have courage to go through with all that is before me."

He longs to give her the desired blessing, it is trembling on his very lips, and yet for her sake he still withholds it.

" Let me first hear you tell your Heavenly Father that you intend to do His will, and cleave to the duties, however hard, that He has appointed you."

"Oh, I do! I swear it," she says solemnly, as, clasping her hands, she raises her pale face and dim eyes to the sky. "I swear before Almighty God, and all the company of heaven, that from this hour I resign all loves, all possessions, all desires, but such as are in accordance with His Holy Will."

"Then may He bless you, my child, may He aid you, may He comfort you, and in His own good time reward you, for the sacrifice you offer up to Him."

He lays his hands upon her head; she hears him breathe a prayer above her drooping form; and then, without another word, rises, wrings his hand, fixes on him a look which, though intensely miserable, appears already to have some peace commingled with its pain, and goes swiftly from his presence on her homeward way.

As she re-traverses the fields and country paths, her whole thought is, what shall she say to Auberon; in what words break to him the resolution she has come to; how write the news he must not fail to know at once. For that she should have the courage to tell her lover she has repented of her word, never crosses Lady Gwynne's imagination; she believes his looks, his agony, his bitter reproaches, would kill her on the spot. Her only idea is, that once within the grounds of Felton Hall, she will creep to her own chamber, and thence, feigning sickness, write and tell him all; and that it is her firm resolve never to see or speak with him again, except as a mere friend. And then when he has gone—for he will go; he is too proud, too tender, too considerate of her feelings—(ah, God, she may not think of all that now)—to stay where it is not desired—she will come again amongst her household, as of old, and strive, Heaven helping her, to do her duty.

But as thus thinking, and shivering slightly from the re-action which has succeeded her fit of terrible excitement, she walks slowly up the dusky carriage drive, she meets Auberon Slade, face to face, and evidently waiting for her.

"My darling!" he exclaims eagerly, seizing her hands in his own. "Where have you been all this time? I have been looking for you everywhere. What have you been doing? Not repenting your promise, I humbly hope," and his laughing eyes, confident, yet tender, seek her own.

But in Gwendoline Gwynne's excited

imagination, she and Auberon Slade are no longer lovers and dear friends, but enemies, avengers, murderers, who would ruthlessly pluck each other's souls from the hand of God, and condemn them to irremediable destruction; and with that thought burning in her heart, she pulls her hands violently from his clasp, and bids him never touch them more.

"Auberon! I take back my promise; I take back everything that I have ever said to you. I shall never be your own."

He retreats from her, almost staggering beneath the unexpected blow her words inflict on him.

"Do you know what you are saying?" he gasps at length, "do you know who you are speaking to? Gwendoline, you have gone mad!"

"No! no! I have been mad: mad to

imagine I had the courage to condemn your soul to everlasting torment—but it is past —it is gone—I am sane again! Oh, Auberon!" in a voice of plaintive entreaty, "be strong! and help me to be strong enough to do my duty."

"I see what you are driving at," he answers; "you have been thinking over the promise you made to me this afternoon, and you have not pluck enough, or love enough for me, to carry it through. Well! if it be so, I have no choice but to submit. I am at your mercy. My happiness, as you well know, is in your hands."

Her heart flutters; she is almost fainting; she raises her eyes imploringly to heaven, and angels gather round her, to administer the strength of which she stands so much in need.

"Auberon! you *know* it is not want of

love for you, and I will not answer so cruel a doubt. . But if you accuse me of lack of courage to fly in my Maker's face, and drag you down to hell with me, I plead guilty. I have not the courage, and I have forsworn the intention; I was on my way to tell you so when we met."

"And so I may consider it *une chose finie,* and that when I leave this place, which I shall do to-morrow, we part, to meet no more, or to meet as strangers, eh?"

"It *must* be so," she whispers hoarsely. "Oh, forgive me for the pain that I have brought upon you."

"Ha! ha! ha! It is rather late in the day to speak of that! It is much as though a man should contract a heavy debt, and being unwilling (*unwilling,* mind you, not *unable*) to pay, plead for pardon from the creditor's hand. But debts of honour are seldom binding, as I am well aware, with ladies."

" Oh, Auberon ! spare me !"

" It is nothing, of course, to mar the happiness of a lifetime—to rifle a heart of its best treasures—to promise to give everything in exchange for so gross a robbery ; and then to plead bankruptcy to suit one's own convenience."

She stands before him, silent but trembling ; her pale, suffering face, upraised to Heaven,—" But you——I thought better of you, Gwendoline !" And as he finishes the sentence, he moves moodily away.

" Oh ! Auberon ! hear me for one moment. I am not changed, nor do I fear ! I feel all that I once felt for you—but God has spoken to me, and I dare not disobey."

" Then you are quite resolved to disappoint me ?"

"I am quite, *quite* resolved to do my duty, for your sake as well as my own! It tears my heart to have to say such words to you—I would rather die than tell you so, but I have no choice—*I cannot damn you and myself!*"

But he will not see it, he will not hear it, he walks impetuously away, and leaves her standing there alone.

"*Auberon!*"

It is like the cry of one in his death agony—it rings through the foliage of the long, deserted avenue; it forces him to whom it is addressed to turn and look at her once more,—"Oh! my love! my love! don't part from me like this."

She holds out her arms towards him—she presses her face against his own—she stamps mad impassioned kisses, born of despair, upon his eyes, and mouth, and forehead.

"Oh! God's best blessings rest upon you. God bless your heart, your soul, your intellect. God keep you safe and make you happy! and return your love for me fourfold into your bosom. Oh! Father! leave me in my misery, desert me, condemn me to everlasting torture, so Thou but stay with him, and bring him to eternal life."

"And yet you will not stay with me yourself," he whispers, as their wet cheeks touch each other.

"I cannot—I dare not—*I have sworn it shall not be!*"

※　　　※　　　※　　　※　　　※

> "O then, like those, who clench their nerves to rush
> 　Upon their dissolution, we two rose,
> 　There—closing like an individual life—
> 　In one blind cry of passion and of pain,
> 　Like bitter accusation ev'n to death,
> 　Caught up the whole of love and utter'd it,
> 　And bade adieu for ever."

※　　　※　　　※　　　※　　　※

They gaze in one another's faces, wildly, hopelessly, fearfully, for the space of a few seconds, and then, as though the sight and the recollections it engenders, were too much for him, Auberon Slade bursts from her, and walks rapidly away ; and she, with her thoughts fixed half on earth, and half in heaven, and murmuring, " Oh ! Auberon ! —Oh ! Christ !" falls unconscious on the spot where she has parted with him.

4—2

CHAPTER III.

THE PRESENTIMENT FULFILLED.

AN old woman who has been gathering sticks and chips for fuel at the further end of the avenue, and is hobbling towards the servants' hall to receive what scraps the cook may have to give her, comes upon the body of Lady Gwynne lying prostrate at the foot of a tree, and giving the alarm in the stable-yard, in another minute half-a-dozen stout arms are ready to carry the mistress of Felton Hall into her own chamber, and lay her on her bed, but half conscious of what has befallen, or is yet befalling her.

And so for many succeeding hours she lies, apparently indifferent to all that passes round her, not stirring even at the sound of Sir Lyster's dreaded voice, as he noisily, and somewhat angrily, demands of her attendants "what the deuce is the meaning of it all;" nor attempting to return the kisses that her child presses so fervently upon her passive cheek.

She sees, as in a dream, the misty figures that move about her bed; hears the con-jectures that are whispered as to the pro-bable reason of her illness; is conscious of being pressed to rise, to take refreshment, or to answer the questions put to her; and yet she lies there, silent and unresponsive, too crushed by her load of misery to care what happens to herself or others.

And then Dr. Stewart is summoned, who, divining from her general condition that Lady Gwynne has undergone some great excitement, ascribes it all to Sir Lyster (whose conduct to his wife has, more than once, been made the county talk), and orders her complete rest and solitude in consequence, for which his patient is proportionately grateful to him. But towards the close of the next day, she becomes feverish and restless, and appears anxious to learn what is happening downstairs during her absence.

"Did any one call this afternoon, Bennett?" she demands of the loquacious lady's-maid who is attending on her; "I thought I heard the sound of carriage-wheels."

"Not as I know of, my lady," rejoins the servant, "but some of the gentlemen as have been staying here, went away.”

“ Which of them ?” in a very low tone.

“ Mr. Penryhn, my lady, and Mr. Slade. They had the dog-cart as far as Leighton Station, and the spring cart took over their luggage. John, he told me over night, as Mr. Penryhn had ordered the carriage for himself; but Mr. Slade, he don’t seem to have made up his mind till this morning, quite sudden like. Sir Lyster drove them over; he seemed terrible put out to be sure, to think they was going. There’s only Sir John and Lady Cleaver, and young Mr. Norris, left now in the house !”

“ Quite a clearance, isn’t it ? Bennett ! did—did you see the gentlemen before they went this afternoon ?”

“ Well, my lady, I did happen to be on the stairs as they was going down—for I thought I should like to have another look at Mr. Slade, who is such a pleasant spoken gentleman, and has always conducted himself like a gentleman to me." (Bennett wishes to intimate here, that Auberon Slade has tipped her liberally for carrying notes to her mistress, but Lady Gwynne is too sad to smile at the dubious compliment her words imply); " but he didn't seem quite himself to-day, to my mind. He looked pale and hurried-like, and whisked down the stairs at that rate, he was gone before I could draw my breath. Sir Lyster, he says to him, when he had his foot on the very step of the dog-cart, ' Do think better of it, Slade !' he says, ' and stay.' But Mr. Slade, he just shook his head—so—and jumped in. And then they drove off, and that's the last I see of him ; but I'm sure the house won't be the same now

he's gone. He was such a merry gentleman !"

" Please put out the lamp, Bennett,
and take your work into the ante-cham-
ber. I think that I could go to sleep !"

Sleep ! Ah, if this be sleep, God save
us from the pain that keeps us waking !

So it is over then ! past ! gone ! they
shall never meet again, except as friends!
and it is her own hand that has done
it; *her* voice that has parted them for
ever !

Oh ! in that hour of patient uncom-
plaining agony, what a fearful retribution
for an act of virtue, does her regretful
memory become !

Gone forth to his own world without
her ! to learn to gather comfort and encouragement from other smiles, to hang
on other looks, to echo the sighs that

burst from other hearts! Oh, if she could but recall him! In that first hour of knowledge that Auberon Slade has taken her at her word (notwithstanding that, at all risks, she would have remained firm to her resolve), Gwendoline Gwynne is conscious but of one feeling; a deep and unconquerable regret for having driven him from her. She knows that she is wrong; she feels that were he back again that moment, imploring her to retract what she has said, to act against her conscience and the counsel of her friend, to desert her child, outrage her Christian profession and fly in the face of society, she would give the same answer that she gave him yesterday; but with the certainty that, for the time being, temptation is removed out of her way and his, the perverseness of humanity returns, and will make itself felt. She tries to think of Heaven, and the joys she might have forfeited had he remained ; of Mr. Lawrence and his holy, fatherly advice ; of Daisy, who (little cared for by Sir Lyster) would have felt so bitterly the loss of all her mother's care ; but she cannot do it, she cannot fix her mind upon these subjects ; they fade away to give place to vivid torturing recollections of the scenes she has passed through with Auberon Slade, the love she has relinquished, the happiness resigned.

She recalls his image as she has seen it, for three months past, in her morning-room ; her garden ; his own study ; reading, writing, in conversation ; gay, sorrowful, or pensive ; but always—from the very first—sympathetic, loving, and devoted to herself !

Oh! why did she ever meet him?

As the question she has already so often put, both to her own heart and his, re-passes through her mind, there flashes on it, like a streak of lightning, the remembrance, thitherto unheeded, of the presentiment she entertained before she met him, that in some shape or other evil would come of their acquaintance!

She *had* then been warned; she had been cautioned to be careful and circumspect, and she had failed to accept the lesson.

Is this retribution her just punishment? Have their happy meeting, and their bitter parting a meaning in them, after all?

How truly, how wonderfully, has that presentiment been fulfilled! How could she have forgotten it till now!

She recalls the scene, the place, the

actors. The foreshadowing of sorrow and of sin that seems to have been revealed to her, the small attention that she paid to it!

No wonder that his very name—(dear name! how different its characters look to her eye now !)—had power to thrill her, that she feared to meet him, that she said she felt as though some great misfortune were in store for her !

And Major Calvert had asked her *how* she feared it !—how plainly the recollection of his words and looks, as they stood together in the window of the dining-room, returns upon her now—and if it were by death, and she had answered " Yes," she thought it was.

And is she not dead : as good as dead ? Has not the best part of her died, beneath the knowledge of his love, and the impossibility of her enjoying it? What greater trial could there be, than to see a great good, the greatest good in all the world to her, held out for her acceptance, and be compelled to relinquish it. Ah, death, that can only kill the body (so she thinks), would be preferable, a thousand times over, to this mental death of mind, and heart, and energy, that is non-existence without the peace of rest.

But Lady Gwynne is mistaken ; she is still young to the sorrow of the world, or she would know that, whilst she retains faith in him whom she loves, she has not drained her cup of bitterness to the dregs.

The cruellest, the most entire, the most prolonged of separations may be amended, since death re-unites us to all who have gone before ; but when falsehood is made

to do duty for truth, coldness for affection,
and reserve for confidence, what shall atone
for such a bitter change ; for even Heaven
must be powerless to restore the love that
earth has worn threadbare. And as yet,
Lady Gwynne has not this trouble to con-
tend against, for her faith in the faith of
Auberon Slade is boundless—illimitable :
not because she knows herself to be *what
she is,* but because she believes him to be
what he is not.

In her humility, his love for her is a
marvel, a mystery, a blessing to be thankfully accepted, but yet never to cease to
be surprised at. And when he has praised
her looks or actions ; declared her fascinating, bewitching, irresistible, she has
smiled fondly down upon him from the
heights of her superior wisdom, and attri-
buted all the sweet, soft nothings, which

most women would so eagerly have appro-
priated as their due, to *his* goodness, and
generosity, and overweening affection; to
anything, in short, but her own powers of
pleasing him. And for like reasons, she
has undoubting faith in his complete fide-
lity.

He will suffer,—perhaps he will reproach, and think her heartless and un-
feeling; to fear so, is the worst part of her
present trial. But he will never be untrue; she is quite sure of that!

For she has taken this man, who—well
enough as men go—does not possess one
half the genius, or the goodness, or the
generosity, that her love attributes to
him; and placing him upon a pinnacle of
her own raising, has poured forth all the
treasures of her great heart at his feet
in such lavish profusion, that that which

at first dazzled and bewildered him, has become so common, that at the same moment he is angrily resentful against her because she has not given him more.

He commenced by wondering—as well he might—what he had done to gain, and bind so vast an affection to himself; he ends by considering he is injured and aggrieved; nay, more,—insulted, by her presuming to point out his duty, and her own.

There will be another and a fuller climax to the thoughts of Auberon Slade, which he would do well to avoid whilst he can—the conviction that some women's friendship is better worth having, than other women's love; and that he is mad who spurns away too hastily the blessings with which it is specially designed by Providence, we shall comfort and sustain each other in our passage through the world.

Let him call for them in that day, and hear no answer to his call; for sympathy, and union of ideas, and wholesome counsel, and all those helps without which some minds cannot live; but which love alone, without energy, or intellect, or appreciation, has no power to bestow.

Oh, is there no good angel by his side as he pursues his piqued and angry course, to whisper submission to him, and a hope of better things to come? There may be, but his rebellious ears are stopped against the warning.

He laughs at the idea of time and patience; those two friends, who, with the help of God, have power to straighten the most crooked path ; his faith in them has gone : a trial of three months has wiped it out, and thenceforth he will fight the world, single-handed, and alone ! So, in his proud resentment of its usage of him, he declares.

Little does he think that he is about to cast away the weapon that of all others would have served him truest in the con-flict—her strong, indomitable faith in his courage and his worth !

Meanwhile, the tears that fall from her sad eyes throughout the lonely night, are shed only for the pain that she inflicts on him.

She does not dare regret it, for she has a simple, childlike faith in her adviser, which tells her she has done the best for Auberon, as well as for herself ; but she blames continually the weakness and the vanity that has brought him whom she loves, to such a sorry plight !

A desolate future stretches out before her : everything seems black, and gloomy, and uncertain ; but she does not fear the suffering in store for her, she scarcely thinks of it ; her whole mind is absorbed with one idea, — that he may receive strength and courage to bear his part like a man !

And even in those first hours of her crushing grief, the hope will intrude itself that if they strive to be patient, and to endure, for duty's sake, all may come right at last. God, omnipotent and omniscient, can make it, if He so chooses ; and how sweet will be the reward that has been earned by suffering, and crowned by His approving smile.

And so, at last she sleeps, with the tears wet upon her cheeks, and his favourite words upon her lips :—

> "———— Wait! my faith is large in Time,
> And that which shapes it to some perfect end."

Sleep on! poor weary heart! Sleep whilst you may; the grief you carry, is nothing to that which is to come. But angels are watching, lest your strength should falter.

Were one of them to speak, and tell you now, that the man whom your affection has almost deified, is shallow, selfish, unworthy of your love, would you believe him?

No! you will trust nothing but the evidence of your senses; scarcely that.

Sleep on, then! it is not for long; the

dreary dawn is breaking, and the moment for your awakening will soon be here !

*   *   *   *   *

CHAPTER IV.

A FRESH ALARM.

ON the following day Lady Gwynne is down-stairs again, moving about her household as usual; rather pale and languid, perhaps, but, to all outward appearance, anxious for nothing, except to atone to her few remaining guests for her enforced neglect of them, and to avoid all allusion to the cause of her mysterious illness.

At the dinner-table she meets Mr. Lawrence, who, having called rather late in the afternoon to receive tidings of her health, was induced, by the promise that he should see her if he remained, to accept the pressing invitation that Sir Lyster immediately held out to him, to spend the evening with them.

She has scarcely been out of his thoughts one moment since they parted, and he is most anxious to ascertain in what spirit she has borne the trial through which he knows she must have passed. But if Mr. Lawrence thinks to gain any intelligence from the white impassive face opposite to him at the dinner-table, he is very much mistaken, for the state of Lady Gwynne's feelings is not to be guessed from the calm, indifferent air with which she appears to regard everything that passes round her; and it is not until they find themselves standing alone in one of the windows of the drawing-room after dinner, that he fully understands the tempest she has gone through.

Then, after a few common-place remarks upon her illness and recovery, he ventures, in a low voice, to observe—

"I thank God that He has given you strength to do your duty.   You have made a brave beginning, and He will enable you to persevere to the end."

But he is almost frightened at the ghastly pallor that creeps over her face.

"*Brave!* If you could but see me when I am alone!"

"The courage is meritorious in proportion to the suffering. Yes, I know that you have suffered"—(Lady Gwynne is biting her lip hard, to stifle the rising agony in her throat)—"but you have given a gift to God, which, though perhaps the best you had to offer, is still inadequate to express the gratitude you ought to feel towards Him."

"I have given Him *everything*," she answers bitterly. "He can at least demand no more from me. My sacrifice has stripped me bare."

"*Bare*, Lady Gwynne! when you have your child, your Church, still left to you? Oh, shame, shame! Take care lest you tempt Him to put forth His Hand again, and make you acknowledge the blessings still remaining to you."

The evil spirit is conquered : tears are glistening in her eyes.

"Forgive me! Yes, I feel that you are right, and that I am wretchedly ungrateful. I will try, indeed I will, to feel more contented. Only—*it is so hard !*"

He knows how hard, for he has fought a weary battle with sin and suffering himself, but he will not tell her so. At this moment undue compassion is likely

to weaken instead of strengthen her resolve.

"When that thought intrudes itself, my
dear friend, call Daisy to your side, and
try to picture what life would be to you
without her. I know of no better advice
to offer, nor remedy to suggest."

And before many days are over, Lady
Gwynne has reason to recall his words.
The first diversion to her melancholy, is
caused by Sir Lyster insisting that the
whole of her illness is attributable to her
going to Church on week days, and refusing to listen to any argument, or reason
on the subject.

"Stewart told me himself, that your
attack was due to over-fatigue and excitement, and I should like to know what
excitement you can find in Felton, unless
it be running to church at all hours of

the day. I never liked the custom. It has been highly inconvenient at times, both to my friends and myself, and I forbid your doing it for the future."

"Oh, pray, Lyster! think what you are saying. It has been such a comfort to me."

"Comfort! Humbug! Church once a week is enough for anybody; and if you want to say your prayers oftener, why can't you say them in your own room? What's the particular good of praying before a bit of brass, and a couple of candlesticks? and if you must have them, why don't you light a pound of dips upstairs, instead of risking your health by exposure to a damp evening?"

"You know it is not that!"

"I'm sure I don't know what it is, then, unless it's part of your religion to run exactly counter to your husband's wishes."

She could have told him what it was; the irresistible attraction of a saving doctrine, which had drawn her, as his cold creed would never have had the power to do, from pleasant sin to the practice of unlovely virtue; which, in teaching her that faith without works is dead, had made her put her shoulder to the wheel; arrested her footsteps on the very brink of vice; and restored her to the arms from which he (blind fool, and undeserving of the effort made on his behalf) is doing his best, once more to thrust her.

"A woman of your age," he goes on testily, "and a mother into the bargain—it's perfectly absurd that you should go playing tricks with yourself, as though you were seventeen. Pray, do you remember how long we have been married?"

"Perfectly!" with a deep sigh.

"Oh, you sigh, do you? You choose to consider yourself ill-used, because your husband takes the trouble to see that you don't ruin your health, and waste your time over such follies. You are going to act martyr for the benefit of the whole family, I suppose, and pretend you are kept prisoner in the house against your will! If this is part of Lawrence's confounded teaching, the sooner he leaves off preaching sermons to you, the better."

"Mr. Lawrence has never taught me anything but good," indignantly; "he is the best friend I have."

"Well I advise you to make the most of the lessons you have received from him, for you've heard the last of them, at all events on week days. Lawrence is a very good fellow at the dinner table (I've no complaint to make of him there), and an excellent partner at piquet, but if he's going to teach you to set up your will in opposition to my wishes, the sooner we see his back the better!"

"He never did!"

"Don't answer me! You've heard my orders, and you'll please to remember them. No more psalm-singing on week-days."

"Oh, Lyster! you cannot be in earnest. I will never permit it to interfere with my duties or your pleasures; but say that I may go sometimes, just when no one wants me, and there is nothing else to do. It is such a comfort at the close of a long weary day to creep into church, and hear the service read."

But the mere entreaty turns his anger into rage.

"No such thing! I won't listen to it! Have I not already expressed my wishes on the subject? D——n it all, Madam, one would imagine that your hearing was as defective as your sense. You've chosen to lay yourself up with your confounded folly, and you must take the consequences of it."

"I have told you already that it was *not* going to church that made me ill."

"And I have told you that it *was!* And I tell you now that it shall not be so again. Do you understand me? or am I to be forced to lock you up in your own room and disgrace you before the household?"

"You could scarcely disgrace me more than you are doing, now when you talk so loud that every one must hear you."

"Let them hear me! I raised my voice on purpose! I wish them to hear me! And if you give me another speech like the last, I'll call all the servants, to bear witness that I intend to be obeyed by you."

Her lip curls, but she answers nothing.

"Ah! I've frightened you at last, have I? I thought I'd let you know which is master. Well! Now I've given you the lesson, I'll leave you to digest it. Good-bye," and as he concludes, Sir Lyster, with a mocking salutation, leaves the room.

She does not rise for a moment after his departure, but when she does so, it is steadily.

"*Fear you!*" she ejaculates, with a look

of withering scorn on the closed door through which he has disappeared. "No! *Husband,* I do not fear—I despise you. Wretched, paltry nature! I can read you plainly now by the light of a superior strength, and wonder how I ever could have been afraid of you! You—who fear yourself, to cross weapons of argument with one of equal strength, yet have sufficient courage to oppress a helpless woman in the security of her own chamber; who would bully a servant, kick a dog, strike a horse—and yet cower silent before your fellow-men. I take shame to myself but for one remembrance — that I was ever coward enough to shrink before your anger; or permit your petty tyranny to embitter my existence. Henceforth, you may storm, flatter, oppress, or compliment; it can make no difference in my feelings towards you. My outward submission must be yours—make the most of it, for you will have nothing more; in earning my contempt, you have cast away the last remaining particle of my affection. Oh, Auberon! is it thus that he would aid me to forget you? Is it for treatment such as this, that I have thrust your dear arms away?"

The bitter remembrance brings tears, and the tears, penitence—but the feeling with which Sir Lyster has inspired his wife that day, will never wholly pass away.

You may provoke a woman's anger, jealousy, indifference or disdain, and find a cure for your shortcomings; but once rouse her contempt; do something which, in her eyes, sets you beneath herself, and all the tenderest emotions of her heart; and she will never forget it. For her nature is to look upwards, and to adore; and the writhing reptile which she spurns indignantly, is never afterwards forgiven for having put her foot to such base use.

The knowledge of this, haunts Lady Gwynne; it distresses her. To shudder at his touch; to feel a weight when in his presence; to despise his opinions, and be indifferent to his welfare, is a grievous sin against the man whom she has sworn to honour, and the God who linked her to him; and yet she cannot shake the rebellious spirit off.

She finds herself comparing everything he says and does, with what Auberon Slade would have said and done, under similar circumstances, and of course, unfavourably—and then she tries to make up for her secret want of faith, by a forced exhibition of interest, and hates herself for the duplicity.

She is open and true by nature; strong in the knowledge of her desire to do right, and fearless of consequences which would fall on her head alone: and did she, at this period, follow the dictates of her heart, would cast herself at her husband's feet, and make an honest confession of the weakness into which she has been betrayed.

But she has not only herself to think of; there is Daisy and there is Auberon— both ready to suffer for her ill-doing— and she dares not contemplate the consequences of such an act to them. Sir Lyster would not forgive her fault, there is little doubt of that; for he has not the capability of according a free and generous pardon. His heart is far too small; his mind too narrow; and last, though not least, his sense of religion, and of his own need of forgiveness, too feeble, to admit of his doing anything so Christian and God-like. For herself, she would neither expect nor demand it; but what would happen to Daisy and Auberon, if the child were deprived of her presence, and the man once more possessed of it?

No! she has struggled so far, and she must struggle on farther, and accept her unwilling reticence as part of the punishment due to her sin. Ah! the punishment falls heavy, even in those early days!

The loss of Auberon's presence; the silence, the blank, the aching void; are as nothing compared to the knowledge that she has caused him to sin, and burdened her own soul, as she believes, for ever !

God, and her heart, alone can guess what she passes through in those first hours of sorrow, feeling that she must, not only resign the one man, but cleave to the other, in thought as well as deed; and yet deprived (by his unnecessary harshness) of the means by which she would have become soonest reconciled to her unhappy fate. She believes at first, that this last evil may be remedied, that she will be justified in taking it into her own hands, and claiming her right to join in the services of the church, when and how she pleases ; and when she submits the matter to Mr. Lawrence, his answer disappoints her, for his advice is, that she shall wait.

" Wait ! my child ! wait and pray ; and

in time this cloud is sure to pass from you."

"But the prohibition is so unjust, so mean, so evidently given with the intention to annoy me."

"That is why I am certain that it cannot last! God permits the sufferings that arise from sin, to continue sometimes for years, because the removal of them might revive the same error; but I never knew Him fail, to step forward to succour those who are deprived through tyranny of the means of worshipping Him! Trust to Him, Lady Gwynne; be patient, regard this unjust deprivation as part of your cross, and whatever else remains, He will remove it. You may take my word for it."

She takes his advice and acts upon it; but she suffers tenfold in consequence, and Providence, in its tender care, lest she should sink into despondency, opens another outlet for the distraction of her mind; Daisy becomes considerably worse!

The results of the serious fall which the child experienced, the immediate effects of which seemed to have been relieved by a few weeks' rest and attention, are about to make themselves felt; her brief respite from pain and weakness is suspended; the worst symptoms return, and Dr. Stewart, after a fortnight's close attendance, asks to speak to Sir Lyster alone, and informing him that he fears some great injury has been done to the spine, expresses his disinclination to do anything further of his own judgment; and advises him to take his daughter to London, and there submit her case to the best advice he can procure.

Sir Lyster is very averse to the idea, and inclined to believe that it is not at all necessary. He entertains none of those weak and foolish fears respecting an only child, of which some fathers are guilty; indeed, unless the truth is unwillingly forced upon him, he seldom remembers that he has a child at all. He takes no pride in the possession of his little girl, although she gives promise of great beauty; he was disappointed at her birth, because she was not a boy; he has been disappointed ever since because she has not had a brother; and her presence disagreeably reminds him of both facts.

Besides, she is tall, and strong, and stout of her age, and Sir Lyster cannot realise that she may be laid upon her back, a hopeless invalid, for the term of her natural life, and is never very ready to produce money which is required for any thing but his own pleasures.

"Go to London at this time of the year!" he exclaims, "with Christmas close at hand, and the place a mass of fog—why, it is out of the question."

"If you value your child's health, you will consider nothing but the necessity of her having immediate assistance."

"But, hang it! it can't be so bad as all that! Why, she was running about a week ago!"

"Symptoms have manifested themselves during the last two days, which make me regret I ever gave my sanction to her quitting the recumbent position."

"Well, she can be kept on her back as much as ever you choose; the more the better, I say, for she is always in mischief when below stairs."

"Mere rest would be now unavailing ; the mischief has gone too far."

"At all events it can do no harm to put off our visit to London till after Christmas."

"Sir Lyster Gwynne ! if you would not see your daughter crippled for life, you will take my advice, and go directly. The necessity is imminent; after Christmas may be too late. I greatly fear there is serious injury done to the spine, although to what extent I am unable to say. If you will not move from Felton, you must send for Pollock, or Aberystwith, or some one skilled in these complaints, and let him see the child at once. But, in my opinion, it will be a long affair, and she had best be on the spot."

Thus seriously admonished, Sir Lyster thinks it best, for the sake of policy, as well as decency, to do as Dr. Stewart desires him, and, consequently, Lady Gwynne is ordered to see all things put in readiness for their departure. But he grumbles terribly over the necessity, nevertheless.

"Such absurd nonsense! at this time of the year, and for a girl, too! Don't believe that old fool Stewart knows a bit about his business. We'll go to town, but if I find he's led me on a wild-goose chase, I'm whipped if I won't dismiss him the minute we return home. He shall never show his face here again. And I should like to know what *I* am to do with myself in London at this season? There'll not be a man of my acquaintance left in town. If that obstinate mule Slade hadn't insisted upon leaving Felton so soon, we might have persuaded him to pass his

Christmas there with us.   As it is, of course he's in Blankshire ! hang it ! everything seems to go wrong in this world !"

How surprised Sir Lyster Gwynne would be, could he divine that, for the fact which appears so much to aggravate his annoyance, a thanksgiving, even in the midst of her anxiety for her child's welfare, is rising from the inmost depths of his wife's suffering soul !

CHAPTER V.

UNEXPECTED VISITORS.

POOR little Daisy is very patient under her misfortunes; children usually are so. She bears the weakness and the pain with a submission that astonishes those who have known her only in her wild boisterous moods, and touches to the quick her mother's heart. For Lady Gwynne is ever by her side; night nor day does she permit any other hand to minister to her child's wants. At the call of this new anxiety, she shakes off the sloth and apathy that have of late oppressed her spirit, and rises to the occasion grandly, bringing all her energies to bear upon it, as though there were nothing else to try her fortitude. She cannot fail to look upon it as a fresh calamity; she little thinks that it comes straight from Heaven, a blessing in disguise.

For it lifts her out of herself, and the too fond contemplation of her feelings; it causes her to raise her eyes from the dead pleasures, lying strewn upon the earth like shaken autumn leaves, and sodden with her tears, and compels her to acknowledge (as Mr. Lawrence prophesied that time might compel her), that she has still some treasures left to lose. It kindles a new fear in her breast, invests her with a new belief, in other hopes and other joys, than those which are linked with her relinquished love; and her mind, full of Daisy

and the probable duration of her illness,
has no leisure to sit down with folded
hands, and mourn the unforgotten Past.
The wound still gapes; how could it be
otherwise? a sword-thrust is not healed in
a day; but it must gape, and bleed now
whilst she goes on her way, unheeding,
with scarce a moment she can call her own
to stop and look at it, and touch it shrink-
ingly, and wonder if it ever will be cured.

It may seem a little mercy to be driven
out of one grief by the immediate necessity
for conquering another; but there is a
sterner trial in store for Lady Gwynne,
a wound that shall divide not only flesh
and bones, but heart and spirit; and by
this temporary distraction, she is gaining
strength to meet it. It is as the lull before
the tempest, or the interval of rest between
the fiercer throes of pain; by it she will

learn to become strong ; without it, trouble might engulf without ennobling her.

So Daisy's mother is transformed to Daisy's nurse ; and the child wonders why she should seem fonder of her than she ever did before, and hang over her bed with such tender looks, calling her "her only hope, her only blessing, God's best gift to her," and thinks, if this be the result of illness, she would rather never get well again.

In a short time after the issue of Dr. Stewart's decree, Felton Hall is emptied of its inmates. Sir John and Lady Cleaver, (who had fully intended spending their Christmas with the Gwynnes,) being very full of sympathy for their friends' misfortune, but still more so for their own—and young Mr. Norris (who is a great chum of Auberon Slade's, and consequently rather a favourite with my heroine) accompanying his host and hostess to London, where, having seen them established in the hotel, they customarily frequent on their visits to town, he leaves them to return to his chambers in the Temple.

The first few days of change are unsatisfactory; for, notwithstanding all their precautions, the invalid has borne the journey badly, suffering much pain in consequence; and the time of the famous physician, Dr. Aberystwith, being so much engaged that he cannot visit her for a week after he has been summoned, her mother's every moment is employed in striving to soothe the weariness engendered by confinement; a task which is not lightened by the ill-humour which Sir Lyster displays at the loss of his wife's society.

But at last there comes a diversion in

her favour ; the great doctor's visit has been paid, and although he hums and haws over Daisy's injured spine, refusing to pronounce a definite opinion at that early stage of the proceedings, and enjoins the strictest rest until he shall see her again, he recommends several things to soothe her pain, and alleviate the tedium of her condition. And with her child more cheerful and at ease, Lady Gwynne's spirits even seemed to revive a little ; and although her inclinations would prompt her to remain quietly at home, in gratitude to Heaven, she puts compulsion on them, and forces herself to comply with her husband's wishes, that she should accompany him to various places of entertainment.

It is now close upon Christmas day, and about a month since she parted with Auberon Slade. London is empty and dull in the extreme, and an occasional drive through the muddy and foggy parks in the afternoon, or a box at the theatre in the evening, are all the amusements the town is capable of affording her.

It is a heavy heart she drags with her to those theatres, and a pale sad face with which she gazes at the depressing farces and weary spun-out dramas; but Sir Lyster enjoys the play, so long as it is something that he can easily understand, and she (notwithstanding that the contempt with which he has inspired her, is always there in its full force, to make her sicken of his company) feels that she owes him something in return for the unfaithful past, and is glad to be able to discharge a small portion of her debt, though at the cost of so large a penalty as this is to herself.

It hurts her, even more than there is

occasion for, to leave the dear child, who is growing paler and thinner with each day's seclusion, to spend the long evenings on her couch alone ; but she does it, almost cheerfully, trusting, that in consideration of the sacrifice, and the reason for which she makes it, her place by Daisy's side will be filled by a guardian more tender, trusty, and watchful than even her own mother can be.

But the days are hers. Sir Lyster has his club, and a few associates left in town even at that season, and generally leaves her for the afternoon alone. And these hours she spends a close prisoner at her child's side, clinging to her, praying over her, entreating her to love her best of all the world, that she may lean upon the happy knowledge that one heart is lawfully and entirely her own.

And whatever meaning the wild incoherent words she often utters, may convey at that period to Daisy's understanding, they sink in and dwell there, and lay the foundation of that deep enduring attachment which ever afterwards exists between the mother and the daughter.

A child may not comprehend the cause of grief, but from its infancy it recognises its effects, and (with some prophetic instinct, perhaps, of what must come to it in after days), sympathises with them. Men and women may scoff at tears, but little children never do. Their tender souls have too freshly come from the hand of God, not to be the first to take part with those that mourn.

So Daisy's ignorant, but ready sympathy comforts her mother, making her almost believe the husband's sins atoned

for, by the child's affection. She is thus engaged one dull afternoon in the first week
in January, when a servant, entering ab-
ruptly, informs her that a gentleman,
Mr. Slade by name, is in the reception-
room below, and will be glad to speak
to her.

At his name, pronounced thus indifferently, and without previous warning, her
cheeks commence to pale and flush. At
the knowledge that he is there, close to
her, only waiting for her appearance, her
very heart appears to stop its beating.

Her first impulse is to rush into his
arms—her next, to say that she is not at
home, engaged, unable to receive visitors—
her third, to remember that Auberon Slade
is still her husband's friend and hers ; and
that after the prolonged and intimate stay
he has made at Felton Hall, she can hardly,

with propriety, refuse to descend to the drawing-room, and exchange a few words with him now.

And the last conclusion is strengthened by the entreaties of Daisy, who has had great kindness shown her by Auberon Slade at the commencement of her illness, and hails the knowledge of his advent as a diversion to the monotony of her present existence.

"Oh! is it really Auberon—dear Auberon, mamma? How kind of him to come and see us! I don't think he can know how ill I am. Do ask him to come up-stairs and see me before he goes again!"

"I will, darling, yes, I will," returns her mother, in strangely hurried tones, as she rises to her feet, and under pretence of arranging her hair afresh, spends some minutes before the mirror, whilst she strives to overcome the sudden weakness that seems to have assailed her.

"How long you are, mamma! Your hair is quite tidy; why should you stay to do it all over again? And Auberon will be tired of waiting—ah, do make haste. He might go away before you get down stairs, and I want to see him so much."

The little plaintive voice has more power over her than her own cowardice.

"I will go, Daisy—I am quite ready now. And I will be sure to bring him up to see you before he leaves again."

She kisses the child hastily, and quits the chamber, but she is obliged to halt upon the gloomy staircase, and try to calm down the agitation that is knocking at her heart.

Oh! why has he sought her out again

so soon ; it is thoughtless, careless, cruel of him ; he might have given her just a little longer, in which to school herself to meet him as a friend.

Yet as she puts the question, her deceitful heart is bounding under the idea that he has found it impossible to stay away.

She did not know he was in town, for since his hurried departure from the Hall, one short note, in which he thanked Sir Lyster for his hospitality, and desired his kind remembrances to Lady Gwynne, is all the news they have received of Auberon Slade ; and she wonders if, having heard of their arrival, he has left Blankshire on purpose to encounter them.

But she cannot stop to consider ; if she delays much longer he will think she has not the courage to confront him, so, casting speculation to the winds, and carrying a heart of which she can count every pulsation, Lady Gwynne hastily traverses the remainder of the flight of stairs, and, without further deliberation, turns the handle of the drawing-room door.

The apartment is full of people, or so it seems to her bewildered gaze; but in another moment she can see more clearly, and discerns the figures of three ladies and an old gentleman, who have risen from their chairs to greet her, whilst she, imagining there is some mistake, is backing out again.

"Lady Gwynne, I believe?" inquires the gentleman, courteously.

"Yes—yes—I am Lady Gwynne—I thought—that is to say, I was told——"

"I am afraid that we must introduce ourselves, my old friend, Sir Lyster, not being at home. I am Mr. Slade—(I think you must have heard my name from my son Auberon)—and this is my wife, Mrs. Slade,"—intimating a very fat old woman, who immediately waddles forward to present her hand—" and these are my daughters, Margaret and Emma. I am so sorry to think we shall not have the pleasure of meeting my old friend Sir Lyster, this afternoon."

She sees it all now—understands how (either by the servant's, or her own stupidity) the mistake of her having heard but one name, has occurred—and proceeds to make the best of it. How mad! how foolish of her to imagine for a moment that *he* would seek her presence again without a word of encouragement to do so!

Her face turns very pale beneath the

inevitable disappointment, and her lips quiver; but she says all that is polite and kind, to Mr. and Mrs. Slade, and in another minute the whole party is re-seated, and engaged, in what would appear to a bystander to be, a most animated and interesting conversation.

They are very different—father, mother, and sisters—from what she had anticipated (how seldom do the relations of our idols come up to the standard we have raised for them!), but they seem honest, kindly people, though rather homely, and her heart warms to them for his sake.

The mother is short, stout, and rosy; so is each of the daughters, in her younger, fresher style; in Mr. Slade alone, a slight wiry old man, with finely cut, and rather prominent features, does Lady Gwynne trace any resemblance to Auberon; and it is to him therefore that she directs the larger portion of her conversation.

"We were only made aware yesterday, through the medium of our young friend Mr. Norris, of your proximity to us," says Mr. Slade, after the mutual surprise of each party, that the other should be found in London at that season of the year, has been expressed, "or you may be sure we should have sooner availed ourselves of the opportunity of thanking Sir Lyster and yourself in person, for the great kindness you have shown our son."

"Oh! pray don't mention it!" replies Lady Gwynne, with the faintest of smiles. —She is longing to ask if Auberon is also in town, but she dares not trust herself to pronounce his name.

"Most flattering, I am sure! most unparalleled, and never to be sufficiently acknowledged," puts in Mrs. Slade with a gratified murmur, "and coming from Sir Lyster Gwynne too ; such an old acquaintance of Mr. Slade's. Auberon's letters were full of it ! and I am sure that to this moment, he feels he never can repay ——"

"I can assure you, there is no obligation in the matter, unless it be on our side. Mr. Auberon Slade's talents are too well known, and his society too much sought after to—to—" but here her voice fails her, and the rest of the sentence is lost in a stifled cough.

"I am afraid you are not very strong," observes the old gentleman, as he notices the painful discomposure of her address. "I trust that this visit to town has not been undertaken on your account."

"Oh ! no ! I grieve to say, it is entirely on that of my little girl, who met with a serious accident some time since at Felton Hall."

"Oh! not that dear little Daisy I hope, of whom Auberon told us," exclaims Miss Slade, enthusiastically, with clasped hands.

"Yes! it is Daisy! I have no other child," replies the mother sadly.

A general condolence is afforded her, with many assurances that her fears must be futile, and nothing whatever will prove to be the matter with Daisy's spine; and then the conversation works itself round again to Auberon.

"I don't think he can be aware of this," his father observes. "How grieved he will be to hear of it."

"Is—is—Mr. Slade then in London?" says Lady Gwynne, forcing herself at last to make the inquiry, which has been trembling on her pale lips a dozen times.

"Oh, yes!—of course—at this present time you know!" replies Mr. Slade with a look of intelligence, which is checked by another from his wife.

She cannot recall what time it is, unless it be the Christmas season, which is a strange period for the owners of country houses to choose to spend away from home.

"It will not be long before he pays his respects to you, I am sure," continues Mr. Slade, mistaking the reason of her silence. "He would have done so before, had he known you were in London."

"Do you—do you make a custom then, of spending your Christmas away from home? Sir Lyster was exceedingly annoyed that we were compelled, on account of our little girl's illness, to do so this year! It is the first time since our marriage!"

"Oh, dear no! This is quite an innovation. Nothing like spending Christmas in one's own house, and surrounded by home comforts; and indeed we did pass the day there, but you see Master Auberon's business has summoned us to town—"

"He is not ill?"—with rather too much anxiety in her voice.

"Nothing of the sort!—but perhaps— you have not heard—"

"Now! Mr. Slade!" interrupted his better-half authoritatively, "that's suffi- cient. You must leave Auberon to tell his own secrets. I am sure, from all we have heard, and he has written to us, that he looks on Lady Gwynne as one of his best friends, and will make her an early recipient of anything he wishes to be public. I dare say," turning to Lady Gwynne, "that you have seen enough of our young gentleman to know that he would not be over-pleased to find that he had been anticipated in his news."

The words and the manner give her the impression, that Auberon's displeasure is rather feared in the home circle; and that its members would do much, not to provoke it, but she has little curiosity upon the subject. Either he has procured an appointment under government, or the secretaryship to a Member of Parliament (an aspiration he has confided to her); or he is about to bring out a new book; and so long as employment, or success distracts his mind, she will rejoice at it. But it can make no difference to her, or her sad heart; which has not even the small consolation of worldly ambition to recompense it for its loss.

But what would his venerable parents think, could they read the thoughts that are crossing through her brain!

"Of course not!" she replies to Mrs. Slade's remark, with a sweet, indifferent smile upon her face, "who would? and at this season, too, when it is so difficult to find anything to talk of. Have you been to see 'Caste' at the Prince of Wales' Theatre yet, Mrs. Slade? It is first rate; an inimitable specimen of modern drama.—Sir Lyster has been three times."

"Is there no chance of our seeing my old friend this afternoon, Lady Gwynne?" enquires Mr. Slade.

"I fear not, unless you will consent to take us as we are, and remain to dinner. I am sure Sir Lyster would be charmed to meet you again, but he is always at his club in the afternoon, and does not return till seven o'clock."

But the Slades are engaged, *en masse*, to a large party at their friends the Camerons, and find it impossible to accept Lady Gwynne's hospitable invitation.

"The Camerons, of course, having a peculiar claim on us," commences the old gentleman.

"Now, Mr. Slade!" interposes his wife with an uplifted finger, "I have already warned you once."

"Well! well! my dear," deprecatingly, "I was merely going to observe—"

"Too much, Mr. Slade, too much. I feel sure that you will let the cat out of the bag before our visit is concluded."

"Well, at all events the cat is safe for the present," says Lady Gwynne, who is amused at the controversy between the wedded pair.

"You won't have to wait long, Lady Gwynne, you may depend upon that. Auberon is a good enough son in his way, but still—"

"You must be very proud of him," she replies, her breast swelling beneath the knowledge, that she too may claim some right to be proud of his achievements.

"Oh, yes! his friends are very good; they make a great deal of him. But his papa often wishes that he had more taste for a country life. We seldom see him down in Blankshire."

"And now we shall see him less than ever, I suppose," remarks one of the sisters.

"Oh, I don't know that, my dear. It is more than likely that when Auberon is—"

"*Now! Mr. Slade!* you are on the brink again. My dear Lady Gwynne, I must take him off at once, or I shall never hear the end of it from Auberon."

And with a prolonged hand-shaking, and many hopes expressed that they shall soon meet again, and entreaties that she shall visit them down in Blankshire, Lady Gwynne sees the last of her guests.

As they file out of the room, and leave her there alone, she feels her cheeks are burning, and to cool them, stands for a few minutes beside the grimy window, looking down upon the street.

Oh, the bustle, the confusion, and the dirt of the gloomy winter's afternoon; the shoving and the pushing, that goes on in the dark fog, through which the sickly gleam of the early lighted lamps is trying to force itself. How they crowd, and bustle one another; each striving to make his own way, without the least concern how his neighbour fares on hers. It is like a little picture of this selfish world, where, so long as *we* succeed, what matter if our brother break his heart, or fall !

And to think that Auberon Slade, and she are part of the motley crew; and that at any moment, they may encounter one another, and stand once more, face to face. She dares not think of it: she is not yet strong enough. He will not come; surely, he will make any excuse, plead any engagement, sooner than present himself before her, whilst every string of his heart and hers, is still quivering from the rough jar, misfortune's hand has caused them.

And then she remembers Daisy, and returning to the child's side, consoles her for the disappointment of not seeing Auberon, by the assurance that he will soon be there; that Auberon's father had said he would, and that whenever he appeared, her nurse should receive orders to show him up into the sick room.

With a mental reservation, that should that epoch ever come (as perhaps for the sake of etiquette it may), *she* will take good care to hide herself; up-stairs, down-stairs, anywhere, so long as it is in a corner too secluded to let the beating of her heart be overheard.

CHAPTER VI.

UNEXPECTED NEWS.

HOW very differently (in usual) things occur, to the manner in which we anticipate them.

The next day is rather a bright day — speaking comparatively — with Lady Gwynne. It is the occasion for Dr. Aberystwith's periodical visit, and Sir Lyster, who has a wholesome dislike, not to say dread, of doctors, and everything pertaining to them, flies the hotel from the moment he is expected, leaving his wife to receive him by herself.

It is not a pleasant ordeal for the poor mother to go through, for she has begun to lose all hope of hearing a favourable opinion issue from the physician's lips.

For weeks past, she has been hanging on his scanty words, and striving to detect a gleam of encouragement in his solemn looks, without success; and she fears, she can hardly say, what. But to-day her patience is to be rewarded; to-day, after a minute and lengthy examination, he delivers his oracular opinion, that though Daisy's muscular powers have received a severe strain, there is nothing the matter but what complete rest in the recumbent position will rectify.

She must remain on her back, perhaps for several years—in her present state of rapid growth and development it is impossible to say for how long—but care, and time, and strict attention, will, humanly speaking, eventually work a cure.

And to Lady Gwynne, who from Dr. Aberystwith's long silence had begun to suspect that her child might never walk again, or even, perhaps, be taken from her, the verdict comes as a return of hope. What, in her eyes, are the trouble, the confinement, the anxiety, which such a prospect entails on her? What shall they be to her darling, so long as God spares them to each other, and she has the opportunity to lighten her weariness, and support her patience? Nothing! Thenceforth she will herself be Daisy's nurse, and governess, and companion, and mother, all in one: will live by her side: read, work, and play with her, until the dear child shall forget what it is, to murmur that her lot is different from that of others. It is a blessed task that Heaven has designed for her : has pre-ordained, perhaps, in merciful intention, to divert her thoughts from what has gone before. And, any way, she is thankful such a duty still remains to her.

She meets Sir Lyster with a face beaming with subdued gratitude, and is surprised to find that he regards the matter in a very different light. He has felt but little concern at Daisy's accident, and subsequent prostration ; he feels as little now to hear there is a chance of her relief.

If Dr. Aberystwith could have made her well, indeed, at once : have set her on her legs again, and spared him the daily recital of the improvement, or retrogression in her symptoms, he would have been obliged to him, for there would have been an end—or so he thinks—to pale, anxious looks upon the part, and calls upon the time, of Lady Gwynne.

But to hear that the best comfort he can give them, is the intelligence, that after years of solitude and seclusion, his daughter may be able to take her place again amongst her fellow-creatures ; during which period her mother will, of course, be dancing close attendance on her, is, in Sir Lyster's eyes, tantamount to the worst ; indeed, it is questionable, whether he would not have felt less annoyance at the news that Daisy's young career would soon be over ; although, with all his brutality, he is not quite brute enough, when in an ordinary mood, to give vent to so un-fatherly an opinion.

But he throws cold water on his wife's new-born hope, by the observation, that if that is all Aberystwith can do for the child, the sooner they call in some one else, the better; and immediately turns the subject by the announcement that he has got a box for that evening, at one of the theatres, where a new comedy is nightly drawing crowds, and she must order the dinner an hour earlier than usual, and be ready to accompany him.

She would rather—oh! how much rather!—spend this evening, which seems somehow like the close of a Sunday, at Daisy's side, revelling silently in the hope so freshly restored to her, and forming plans for the new life they must begin to lead together—but she does not even hint at it. She only gives a sigh to her relinquished wish, and then prepares to make

arrangements for her child's comfort during her absence with her husband at the
theatre.

The house is crowded ; but Lady Gwynne
sits behind her curtain, gazing abstractedly
at the stage, often but half conscious of
what is taking place upon it, and never
dreaming of inspecting the many bright
faces, and gay costumes, by which she is
surrounded.

Not so Sir Lyster ; who may be pardoned
perhaps at this time for not finding his
wife (however submissive) so lively a companion as she might be, and whose constant raids upon the buffet seem inva-
riably to result in his meeting some one
whom he imagined to be at the other end
of the world.

Lady Gwynne hears of Lord Ashton,
and Denison of the tenth, and Sir Harry

Lorrimore, without exhibiting any violent emotion ; but she is rather startled out of her passive demeanour, when, between the comedy and the final farce, Sir Lyster re-enters the box, with a companion in tow, and she finds herself, face to face with Auberon Slade.

Here—really here—in her very presence ! and she had thought, upon a first encounter, to hide herself, until she had become accustomed to the cadence of the voice which she can no longer call her own.

Oh ! God ! stop this fearful trembling ! She shakes from head to foot, as though she had an ague.

"Thought I'd surprise you !" says Sir Lyster jocularly. "Spotted the fellow half an hour ago, hid in a perfect nest of ladies, and bided my time to pounce upon him. Knew he'd be out for brandy and soda before long. And he says he never heard we were in town until last evening! Are those the morals that you taught him, Gwendoline?"

"Upon my life I didn't," replies Auberon Slade lightly.

At the tone of his voice, she starts, gives a rapid glance towards him, and is still.

What! no tremble, no falter, no confusion! Is it possible that he can meet her thus, and feel no pain? At the bare suspicion, her blood freezes in her veins.

"I hope I see you well," he says next, bending over her, and his face smiles— actually smiles, as he addresses her. "You did well to come to town, though I was very sorry to hear of the cause of your journey. The country must be horribly dull just now, all mud and leafless boughs,

I suppose.   There is really no place like London in which to carry off the effects of bad weather."

She does not answer him; she *cannot,* his indifferent manner is piercing her like a sword.

"Well, Slade, I must go!" exclaims Sir Lyster; "Denison is waiting for me. Shall I find you here on my return?"

"Certainly! if Lady Gwynne will permit me to remain;" and as he speaks, Auberon Slade takes possession of the chair just opposite to her; "it is a long time—let me see how long? why, two months or more, is it not, since we have had a talk together."

Oh! can he—*can* he have any recollection of that last interview in the drive at Felton, if he speaks like this? Yet she forces herself to say something in reply.

"I saw your mother, and father, and sisters yesterday, Mr. Slade."

"Yes! so they told me! Indeed, it was from them, that I heard that we are neighbours. My apartments are in the next street to your hotel."

"We had no idea of that!" she answers quickly; "we always occupy the same rooms, when in town."

"Ah—yes—very convenient—it's a first-rate place to stay at."

"We have no fault to find with it."

"Have you been very gay since coming up?"

"Oh, no! Daisy's condition has been, and is still, exceedingly precarious," and there is just the faintest tremble in her voice, as she remembers how little interest he has evinced upon the subject.

"Ah, yes!—poor little thing!—so I

heard.   But I have been so very gay myself since leaving Felton Hall, that it is difficult to credit my friends have not been the same.   I have been out, night after night—positively"—with a laugh that is intended to be very gay—" I don't believe I have spent an evening at home."

" Indeed ! how charming."

" I was at a tremendous affair last night at the Camerons'.   Perhaps my people mentioned the Camerons to you."

" They did—just mention them."

" They are great friends of ours, awfully rich, and keep first-rate society.   By the way, I have something to tell you about them, Lady Gwynne."

" To tell me ?" with quiet surprise.

" Yes !" and Auberon Slade begins to look just a little awkward, as he diligently affects to be suiting her opera-glasses to his own sight. "Do you remember, when I first went down to Felton Hall, my talking to you about Lady Mary St. Maur?"

"Perfectly."

"What a calf you must have thought me, blabbing my love-affairs to the first person I met. Pshaw! what fools we men do make of ourselves. I wonder how many more *affaires du cœur* I shall have to boast of, before I die! But, if I remember rightly, you promised me on that occasion that, should I ever be in earnest in the matter, I might depend upon your good wishes for my happiness."

"I remember it also."

"Well! I'm really in earnest at last, Lady Gwynne. I've been thinking very seriously about the subject lately, and I've come to the conclusion that it won't do for me to go on any longer, as I'm doing now."

"I don't think I quite understand you."

"I mean——" (how very difficult it seems for him, to make those glasses suit his vision) "that it is quite impossible that I can devote my life to literature, as I fully intend to do, whilst I keep late hours, and lead an irregular existence, and so—so—(what a beastly long time they keep us waiting between the pieces, don't they ?)—well, the fact is—(you say my people told you all about the Camerons ?)—"

"They mentioned that the Camerons had a peculiar claim upon them, but they did not say why."

"Well, the reason's plain enough; it's ecause I've—I've—in fact, I've—there's really nothing else for me to do—I've made up my mind to marry." A dead silence!—there is no obstacle to his completing the explanation he has begun. "And Charlotte Cameron has consented to fill the place. She's a very good kind of girl, who will see that I'm not bothered about household affairs—and make me quite as affectionate a wife as I care to have. In fact, the matter was settled a fortnight ago (I made sure my people would have told you about it); and I believe the wedding is to come off early next month. And there'll be an end to my bachelor existence for ever! Ah, well! there is nothing to regret in it. It has not been a particularly happy one!"

He has been rattling on, in a hurried nervous manner, in order to conceal his want of ease; and now he halts, that she may answer him. But the only answer he receives, is an unbroken silence. The noisy orchestra has re-commenced its *répertoire* of quadrilles, and waltzes, and scraps of operatic overtures, and the hum of voices rises from the pit and stalls below; but between those two, sitting behind their curtains, and opposite to one another, not a syllable is exchanged.

Auberon Slade wishes she would speak; that she would abuse, reproach, revile him; do anything but maintain this frigid, fearful silence. He recalls an hour, long since past at Felton Hall, when he had asked, half in earnest, and half in badinage, what she would do when he was married; and had been almost frightened by the sudden change that came upon her face at the bare supposition.

He glances, almost timidly, in that face now, but no such change has passed upon it, with the reception of the actual news; and yet it looks still more alarming, for they are the features of a statue; cold, fixed, immovable.

"Gwendoline!" he ejaculates in a low voice, but the sad grey eyes, half veiled by their dark lashes, continue to stare straight before them, at the drop-scene and the stage. "I feel there is some explanation due to you, for this sudden engagement on my part," he goes on hurriedly, and experiencing a miserable sensation of discomfort the while; "but to myself, it appeared simply unavoidable. You know all that passed between us; it was quite impossible that it could go on (you acknowledged that yourself); and it seemed to me, that the best means, by which I could crush out the feeling, both in you and myself, was my marriage. That will, of course, put an end to it for ever. *Du reste*, however careless, I am not capable, and never was, of leading the immoral life that some men take pleasure in; and that, sooner or later a wife would become a necessity to me, was inevitable. And, having made up one's mind to a thing, there is no time like the present (philosophers say) in which to execute it."

Still, not a word! Her heart is beating so slowly, and coldly, and laboriously, that each breath feels as though it must be her last; whilst his, is bounding, and throbbing with anxiety, as though it would burst its bonds. Oh! that she would but speak, or cry, or redden, or do anything to make her look more natural. But, for all the emotion she displays, Lady Gwynne might not have heard a word that Auberon Slade has said to her.

"I expected you would blame me," he continues, rapidly opening and shutting the lid of her scent-bottle; "women so seldom view these matters in the same light as men; but you will come to acknowledge, some day, that it is the kindest thing I could have done for both of us. It is not, as if we had the slightest hope of ever being more to one another than we are. And of course it was all very wrong and very sinful; and I was a villain, ever to try to persuade you to think otherwise. It has weighed very heavily on my mind, I can assure you; indeed, I have suffered more, than perhaps you would give me credit for; however, it is all over now, and I have put temptation out of my way for the future! Charlotte will make me an excellent wife—and I hope that I shall never forget my duty towards her."

*   *   *   *   *

"It's awfully hot up in these boxes, is it not? You should tell Gwynne to get you one of those on the lower tier! They are twice as comfortable!"

*   *   *   *   *

"I am sure, if I could make you understand all that I went through, before I arrived at my present conclusion, you would alter your opinion about me! Well!"—with a sigh—"I suppose I must accept that, together with the rest, as a part of my punishment. Ill deeds usually bring their retribution with them!"

*   *   *   *   *

"I wonder if Gwynne is waiting for me to join him! I expect he must be! I had better go and look after him, for there's an uncommonly pretty girl at the buffet outside. I shall see you again, of course, Lady Gwynne! You will permit me to call at the hotel, to inquire after my old friend Daisy ?"

He has risen from his seat, and puts the last question so pointedly, that she seems forced to answer. But she only bows her head.

" We shall always be good friends, I hope," he urges; "we *must* be, not only because there is no reason against it, but for the sake of the past, of our connections, and the eyes of the world. There is no need we should cause an *esclandre*. *Au revoir*, then !" lightly.

Her lips form something, it may be good evening or good-bye, but no sound issues from them.

He pauses at the door, and turns again towards her.   " Gwendoline !"

It is his last appeal, and she receives it, as she has done the others.   He looks at her averted face for a moment, heaves a deep sigh, deep enough to reach her ears, and disappears.

And she still sits where he has left her, with her eyes fixed upon the stage.

Lie down now, broken heart, lie down and rest.   You may still bound, and quiver, and melt, before life's journey is concluded, but the worst is over.   You can never feel more acutely, than you are feeling now !

*   *   *   *   *

" A deuced bad farce this," exclaims Sir Lyster, bursting into the box, a few minutes after the curtain has risen, " and not worth staying for ; everyone says so, so let's go home!   At least, let me put you into the carriage, for I suppose you're ready."

"Quite ready!" she replies, as she rises to her feet, and feebly searches for her various wraps.

"All right then; come along.   Good Heavens! what a time you are.   I've got Slade, and Dennison, and Lorrimore, and half a dozen fellows, waiting for me down below.   I've promised to sup with them at Simpson's."

"I need not sit up for you, then?"

"Sit up! I should think not!—If you get up at a decent hour, you will be in time enough for me.   Now, here's the carriage; don't be the whole night getting in! That's it.   Home!" to the coachman, and as Lady Gwynne sinks back upon the cushions, only anxious to close her eyes on everything connected with this weary world, she catches sight of a gay group of men, clustered beneath the lamplights of the theatre, with cigars between their lips, and light, loud words upon their tongues, amongst which, apparently the lightest and the gayest there, Auberon Slade is conspicuous.

Oh, GOD! that this were death, and life and pain indeed were over!

CHAPTER VII.

THE FALLEN IDOL.

AND yet she reaches the hotel, ascends to her apartments, visits the bedside of her sleeping child, and permits her maid to undress and prepare her for her rest; and through it all, indulges in no look, word, or expression, that shall lead one to believe she has anything of more consequence than usual, weighing on her mind.

Even when left to herself, in the wide gloomy London chamber, without any auditor or witness of her grief, Lady Gwynne gives vent to neither sobs nor groans, but sits bolt-upright in her chair, gazing with a kind of tearless despair at her surroundings, and checking, with impatient pride, the heavy sighs that every now and then, rise labouring from her burthened heart.

I think that some may wonder that this woman, who fell prostrate to the earth when she dismissed her lover, smitten unconscious by the bare knowledge of her resignation, can ponder silently over the reception of, what has been confessed to be far bitterer news to her; a consummation of her sacrifice, as deadly, as it was unforeseen.

But the solution of her conduct, lies in the fact that her happiness was a free-will offering to Heaven, resigned of her own accord—her faith is being torn from her. The first act proved her stronger than she had thought herself to be ; the last is a confirmation of her impotency. And the deep humility, and want of self-reliance, which gave her courage to tear her heart from Auberon Slade, find no place in the feelings with which she contemplates his endeavour to wrench their souls asunder.

Pride supports her !—pride, that he should remember so little of the promises he has made, the confessions he has extracted, as to speak lightly of that, which he knows must be the death of her last hope, the hope of retaining his confidence and affection—to smile in her face, whilst he kills the only chance of happiness he has left remaining to her !

* * * * * *

"Then draw me closer—closer to thee, dear,
 Do what we will, thy fate and mine are fixed,
 Thy life and mine inevitably mixed:
We take our destiny, and do not fear!

> " Yes ! all of self has sweetly died in me,
>   Thy noble heart is beating in my breast ;
>   No one shall steal it now—there, let it rest ;
>   And know, dear love, that I am lost in thee !"

*　　　*　　　*　　　*　　　*　　　*

And she had told him at the time, that those verses could never have been written for herself, that he must have mistaken his feelings, have said more than he intended !

And he had sworn (she can see his tender eyes beaming on her now), that if he were not in earnest then, he had never been in earnest in his life !

Oh, can he be so weak ? is it in mankind to be so pitifully weak, as to forget in a few hours, the emotions which have had power to bring tears to the eyes, and enervate the noblest purposes ?　Can the offspring of repentance, which comes direct from God, be faithlessness ; or a consciousness of wrong give birth to cruelty?

Or—and as this thought comes upon her, Lady Gwynne rises from her chair, and begins to pace the room—or, can it all have been a lie, a base deceit? Can Auberon Slade have stooped to play upon her deepest feelings for the indulgence of his own?

Oh, no! no! *no!* She will believe the worst of him—that he is weak, foolish, cowardly, unfit to battle with the world, or to rise above its troubles—but she cannot believe that he *intended* to deceive her.

Ah! the worst pain is over now. There is no such pain in this world, like the pain of pulling down from its pedestal, the idol we have worshipped there!

She has considered him so noble, so good, so tender-hearted, so far above his fellow-creatures, that it is hard to credit all at once, he is about to prove himself just a little frailer, and less generous, and less godlike, than the generality of men. She has wept for him, and for herself, until the fountain of her tears seems almost dry ; but this last grief—a grief not for her own loss, but her loss of faith in him—conveys too great a shock with it to be relieved by any outward signs of emotion.

Auberon married ! *her* Auberon, who but a few weeks back had told her, that he could not live without her, about to be married, to blend his life with another life —whilst she, she is to be shut out in the cold and the darkness, and to bear no part in that domestic happiness ! No ! she cannot believe it. Disbelief is the next feeling that takes possession of her heart. It is impossible ! it cannot be ! he must have been in jest. What could he have said to any girl to induce her to accept him ?

And then a sudden knowledge of the deceits he must have uttered, the subterfuges had recourse to, the false protestations which must have passed his lips, either to Charlotte Cameron or herself, strikes her imagination—and, with a bitter cry of anguish, Lady Gwynne falls upon her knees, and buries her face in her hands, as though even in solitude, she would not let her looks bear witness to his degradation.

For, with that remembrance, down comes the idol from his pedestal; falling like Dagon at the word of God, and disclosing the feet which had upheld him to be but clay. She loves him—however great her weakness and her sin, her heart is honestly his own, and will be so until her dying day —but he is not perfectly sincere ; bitter as is the truth, she must accept it; she can never set him up upon that pedestal again, and his death would have proved a lighter trial to her.

"Oh, Auberon!" she moans, "would it had been anything but this—and at this moment! God knows, I do not grudge your happiness, if happiness and honour can go hand in hand. But to think that you could *stoop* to this, to soil your lips and degrade your nobler nature for the sake of *any* woman, is the bitterest pill you have yet called on me to swallow!"

She feels no jealousy of Charlotte Cameron, who is as yet a myth to her, something in which she cannot make up her mind to believe, and of whom, if she does think, it is to pity; but her whole mind is absorbed in, and weighed down by, one idea, not that Auberon Slade has deserted her, but that he cannot have deserted her without deserting truth at the same moment.

Would she, in due time, have grudged him the consolation of marriage—she who had driven him from her side, with the fixed determination never to clasp hands again, except in friendship ? Oh, no ! had he permitted years, months, the barest period which would have permitted him to say with truth that he could love again, to elapse, she would have been the first to rejoice at the restoration of his peace of mind, and to regard it as an answer to her prayers, and a proof that Heaven had forgiven her share in its former mutilation. But that he should rush at once—fresh from her arms, to those of a stranger—to repeat the same vows, the same glances, the same fond words ; and then be able to look her in the face and tell her calmly, that he had given that, which she had—not scornfully rejected, but at the voice of God, resigned with bitter tears—into the keeping of another—oh! it is not a thing to be argued about. or reasoned over, or palliated; it is a bitter wrong and shame; a wrong to her. whose life is bound up in his own, and a shame to the divine nature which he inherits from the Universal Father!

Does he owe her *nothing* in return for all her tears, her misery, her loss of him, and self-respect, that he cannot place restraint upon himself for a few months at least, and prevent this fresh outrage on her feelings. whilst the cup of bitterness he has helped to fill for her. is yet undrained.

If all that he has said, and done, and sworn to her, is false, can he so early have lost tolerance for her sufferings, as to take pleasure in their augmentation?

She tries to compare the Auberon of last night, with the Auberon of six weeks before, and feels as though she were going mad beneath the effort.

*   *   *   *   *

> "O! idol of my worship! far too fair
>> In the great soul that flashes from thine eyes,
>> I triumph, that I win so great a prize,
> I tremble, when I think how much I dare."

*   *   *   *   *

Is it,—could it have been Auberon Slade who wrote those words, and told her they were true? Oh, yes! she knows it was, and that whatever he feels now,—whether he is fickle, changeable, and inconstant, or has too soon forgotten, or tired of, the past, he loved her once. He loved her when his eyes so tenderly melted into hers,—when his hand sought her own,—his head rested on her bosom; she shall never forget, nor cease to believe in that; and her last thoughts that night are all tender excuses for his conduct, and determination to shield it from the world.

"Thank God," she thinks, "that no one knows of all he said to me : that not even to Mr. Lawrence have I betrayed his name. My poor Auberon! who knows what temptations and difficulties may not have beset his path; 'twere hard if all his friends turned against him as I have done. Perhaps he thinks he is acting for the best, for the kindest, towards me and himself. Any way, if he is all wrong, or untrue, or cowardly, the consequences of his error shall not be aggravated by me.

"Who am I, to find fault? I, who would have dragged him down to the lowest depths of Hell! Oh! my love!"—

with her pale face raised to Heaven—" you have nothing to fear from me. I, who deserve less than nothing at your hands and Heaven's. Be happy if you can ; my misery cannot be increased by seeing you at peace.

" Yet, oh ! my God ! if I could but be convinced that when he said he loved me, he was, at least, deceiving himself, as much as he was deceiving me !"

Aye ! it is there the arrow presses home : there that the weak flesh shrinks from the poisoned barb : the fearful doubt of his sincerity. And in this hour of suspicion Gwendoline Gwynne would bear twice the pain that she is bearing, to be assured that her beloved has not proved false to himself.

But there is no voice to answer her, and she is not in a condition to appeal to others' judgment ; she can only rest upon the memory of bygone days, and with a woman's strong, unreasoning faith, believe that such things *are,* because she wishes them to be.

And even so, with her short, sobbing breath, and broken slumbers, she is happier than the man who has attempted to deceive her ; for, shut his eyes as he may to the truth, and delude himself with the ideas that " what can't be cured, must be endured," and " one woman is as good as another," the memory of her sad eyes, and eloquent silence, haunts Auberon Slade throughout that night's revel, as they will haunt him for many years to come.

But he has chosen his lot : let him abide by it. The lot that has been chosen for her, may prove the happier of the two.

And yet she has done nothing to destroy his faith in her!

Ah! poor, bewildered, and forsaken Gwendoline!—forsaken, though not comfortless—who shall unravel the mystery of God's dealings with the children of men!

CHAPTER VIII.

HIS FRIENDS' OPINIONS.

LADY GWYNNE hears enough of the projected marriage from that time forward; everyone she meets has a remark to make upon the subject, and it seems to her as though, in communicating the intelligence to her ears, Auberon Slade had bellowed it forth to the whole world.

The history of the rise and progress of his courtship, appears to be as well known to his friends as to himself: the day on which he proposed, the words he used, and those in which Miss Cameron answered him, are public property ; and one would think, to hear how freely the topic is discussed, that there is something to boast of, in being hardy enough to fix the destiny of one's whole life in a few hours ; and to swear to love and cherish until death, a creature, for whom you did not care a snap of the fingers six weeks beforehand.

The first instalment of misery under this shape, which Lady Gwynne is called upon to endure, comes from her husband, who can talk of nothing else over the breakfast-table, on the following morning.

"I've got a bit of news for you," he calls out, as soon as she has entered the room.

" Yes ! what is it ?"

" Slade's going to be married ! Ha-ha-ha ! what do you think of that ? Your ethereal poet, who was to live upon air and the sighs of his sentimental admirers, for the term of his natural existence, is going to take to mutton-chops, and buttered muffins, and a four-poster instead. Aren't you disappointed ? Isn't it horribly un-romantic ?"

" He told me so himself last night," she answers quietly.

" Oh ! broke it gently, did he ? Well, it was very considerate of him. I daresay he makes a point of going round, and breaking it gently, to so many head a day. He didn't take half that trouble with me. You had not been gone two minutes, before he asked me to come up to the Camerons' box with him, and be introduced to one of the finest girls out. And so she is—slap-up—and no mistake about it!"

"You went with him; you saw her?" in a slightly anxious tone.

"Haven't I just said I did? Her name is Charlotte Cameron, and she's everything Slade represented her to be—just my style, lots of colour, and lots of flesh! I hate your faded, washed-out, wisps of straws; give me a woman who has something in her!" with rather a contemptuous glance to where his wife—grown considerably paler, and thinner of late, and looking decidedly "washed-out" this morning— has taken a seat opposite to him.

"It has been rather a sudden affair, has it not?" she says next; "at least, I didn't think he had any intention of marrying when he was down at Felton Hall."

She cannot help being curious on the

subject, although each fresh revelation seems to pain her more than the last. She longs so much to hear, or to be able to deduce from what she hears, that Auberon Slade has been caught, entangled, betrayed into this engagement, almost before he knew what was befalling him. But she is not likely to derive that comfort from Sir Lyster.

" Well, you don't suppose he would have told you if he had ? It's only you fools of women who go blabbing your love-affairs to every one. For my part, and from what he said to me last night, I believe it's been on the cards a long time. They've known each other for years ; the Camerons are old friends of the Slades, and there's plenty of money on both sides, so I have no doubt it's been a preconcerted thing ; anyway, all parties seem very well satisfied with it now.   Didn't Slade point Charlotte Cameron out to you ?   A fair girl in a blue dress — uncommonly jolly-looking, that's what I call her."

" No ! he didn't."

" Ah ! he had no scruples with regard to me and Dennison.   It was 'Lotty this,' and 'Lotty that,' till the end of the evening ; and then he treated us to a royal supper at Simpson's.   He's the boy to make the champagne fly, too ; we had such a work to get him home afterwards.   He's a deucedly lucky fellow, that's my opinion ; falling into such a comfortable berth as the Camerons are sure to make for him, at his age, and without the necessity of touching ink and paper again, unless he becomes very hard up for something to do."

" Who are the Camerons, Lyster ?"

" City merchants, I believe —wholesale

tea importers, or something of that sort."

" Not in the same position as himself, then ?"

" Well—they're highly respectable people, and enormously wealthy. They tell me that Cameron's name stands very high in the city; and after all, you know, a man raises his wife to his own position."

" True, if she is capable of being so raised."

" A man of my standing, for instance," resumes Sir Lyster, in his most pompous tone, " might have married anyone. Whatever my wife might have been, in making her Lady Gwynne, and investing her with one of the oldest titles in England, I should have——"

" Yes—yes !—I know !" she interrupts

him hastily. She has heard all this vulgar boasting so often before. But Sir Lyster is not to be cheated out of his due.

"Had it not been so," he continues, " I should have been compelled to look for high birth and breeding, in the probable mother of my heirs."

"My father was a gentleman," she answers quickly. She is always ready to resent any affront cast upon the memory of the poverty-stricken vicar of Ynys-ced-wyn.

"Oh! yes, yes—of course—we all know that; but the world is very apt to judge by outward appearances. The Camerons are wealthy and influential, and the opinion of most people will be the same as mine, that Charlotte Cameron is an excellent match for a man, who intended to make his living by his pen."

" But without the necessity—you say the Slades are also rich."

" Old Slade is not badly off, but he has several daughters to provide for, and I don't suppose that Auberon will come in for much more than the house and grounds in Blankshire. He knows what he is about, you may depend upon it : he's feathered his nest uncommonly well, the young dog ! and got nothing to do with his life, but to enjoy it. I only wish I were he !"

With which complimentary conclusion, Sir Lyster, having finished his breakfast, leaves his wife in peace.

But it is not long before she discovers that opinions run very counter, concerning the great expediency of Auberon Slade's marriage, and that but few of his intimate friends can be found to agree with her

husband. Amongst those most invete-
rately opposed to the idea, is Mr. Norris,
who takes an early opportunity of calling
on her, apparently with the sole reason
of enlarging on the topic, which is so
objectionable to him.

"Lady Gwynne!" he exclaims in the
most despondent accents, as he throws
himself into a chair, "what *is* the meaning
of all this; can you explain it?"

"Explain what, Mr. Norris?"

"This marriage of Slade's. It is the
most imprudent, foolish, mad thing he
has ever contemplated doing in his
life."

"So I should imagine, but Sir Lyster
seems to think that Mr. Slade is a very
lucky man."

"Sir Lyster only looks on the surface;
what can he tell of the effects that a

fatal mistake of this kind is likely to have on a man of Slade's disposition ? Lady Gwynne ! I've known him for years— we were at school, and at college together, and have been firm friends ever since ; we never had a quarrel in our lives ; and I tell you seriously, that this marriage will be the ruin of him ; I know it will. He might almost as well cut his throat at once."

She is surprised at the sudden change in his voice ; and glancing up sees that the kindly young eyes are filled with tears ; and has difficulty in preventing her own from flowing.

"Oh, Mr. Norris ! it is very good— it is very kind of you to feel for him like this : but what can we do ? Mr. Slade is his own master, and not likely to listen to the advice of friends."

"But what is the reason of it? what induced him to make such a fool of himself?"

"How can I tell?" but the deep blush that overspreads her pallid features, joined to the gossip of the Felton smoking-room, in part, betrays her.

"What does he want with marriage at all; I am sure he had no thoughts of it at Felton; he was well enough as he was—and with such a woman too."

"But I hear Miss Cameron has great beauty."

"Beauty! She has *nothing*, Lady Gwynne, positively nothing — neither beauty, accomplishments, talents, nor birth. That's the marvel of it to me. If he had chosen a woman who was remarkable for any one possession—we all know how men are caught, some by feature, and some by talent, and some by grace—but to tie himself to a raw school-girl, who blushes if you are introduced to her—bah! it passes my comprehension."

" She may improve," says Lady Gwynne softly. " She will develop." She does not know what to say, poor creature ; she longs to sit down, and have a good cry herself, but a species of self-imposed generosity forces her to take the part of the absent and the abused.

" Develop!—yes! that she will, into five-and-twenty stone. Your common-bred women always do. Oh, Lady Gwynne! you know the sort of wife, that Slade (if he must have a wife) should have taken to himself. An indolent, careless fellow, fond of luxury and indulgence, and yet without an idea of restraining his expenses ; who must needs, for the sake of his profession, keep open house for men of note and letters; and will require to see that house thoroughly well kept, and made bright and pleasant to his friends, should have placed some one at the head of his table, who was fit to carry out his wishes. But fancy Charlotte Cameron doing the honours of a dinner-table! She is more likely to drive men away from the house, than to attract them to it. I, for one, won't set foot in it, after she is established there."

"But—but—I suppose Mr. Slade has calculated all these disadvantages, and finds that his affection for Miss Cameron out-balances them."

"His affection! Why! do you imagine he is in love with her, Lady Gwynne?"

" Why else should he marry her ?"

" Ah, that I can't tell you! I came to you to solve that mystery, you may remember: but I am quite sure of one thing—that he is no more in love with Charlotte Cameron, than he is with Daisy."

At these words, a spark of pleasure is kindled at her heart, but quickly quenched again. She feels sadly now, that hope, and grief, and pleasure, and all things connected with Auberon Slade, are illegal to her; he has cut her off from them; she is no more, even his dear friend.

" How he ever came to propose to her is inexplicable to me. I suppose he had had too much wine, and does not know how to back out of it now! He asked me to be ' best-man' at the wedding, but I refused. I told him that I would just as soon go and see him hung, as make such an ass of himself. He winced a little at that, but there's nothing like plain speaking."

"Oh, Mr. Norris!" with perhaps a trifle more eagerness in her tone, than is prudent, "don't turn against him! Remember, if he is about to do that which is likely to alienate him from his friends, how much more he will need the few that are left to him. And you have always been such a true, faithful friend to him; you have each received kindness from the other; you will not surely, let such a little thing as this, separate you now."

"Such a little thing! If you knew Charlotte Cameron, Lady Gwynne, you would not call marriage with her, a little thing."

"Well, whatever it may be, the consequences will fall heavier on him than on yourself, and you will not make him feel them worse than he need do! He is so sensitive; he will be so very much alive to the world's ridicule of, or censures on, his conduct, that if you care for him (and I am sure you do), you will not, by unnecessary coldness, increase the load he may have to bear. We have all so much to bear in this world, Mr. Norris!"

"We don't all bring it on our own heads."

"Don't we? I think we do; or that if we do not, it is not our fault."

"One would think you owed him something, by the way you defend his cause, Lady Gwynne!"

She starts so quickly, and looks so pained, that he corrects himself, almost with an apology.

"I mean to say, that—considering all things—so long as he stayed at Felton Hall, and the kindness with which he was received there—I don't think Slade has behaved very well to you and Sir Lyster."

"In what way?"

"Well! if this engagement of his has existed for such a time, he ought to have told you of it."

"Has it so existed?"

"He says that, if not actually settled, it has been in his mind for ages past, and that he always knew that, sooner or later, it would come to a marriage between them, which is the same thing."

"But, Mr. Norris,—surely you know—it was no secret, the fact of his engagement to Lady Mary St. Maur;— *that* was only broken off last season."

"What of it, Lady Gwynne? In these days of rapid motion, when we wear mourning six weeks for our nearest relations; gallop through the Divorce Court when we have been wed a twelvemonth, and marry again before our wives are cold in their graves; an engagement more or less, during the season, is of little consequence. But I think he ought to have made it public. A man has no right to go amongst young girls, passing as free, when his hand is already promised—or nearly so."

"Ah,—well," she answers, with a forced laugh, that would be so gay, that it is infinitely sad, "he had not much opportunity of doing damage at Felton Hall, anyway."

She will defend him no longer; for nothing closes her lips so quickly, as what she takes to be, another proof of his equivocation.

"I fancy, I must have bored you enough on this subject, Lady Gwynne," says Mr. Norris, rising to his feet, "and must ask your pardon, if it has been too much, but my head is full of Auberon Slade at present.

However, I will bear in mind what you say, and try not to make things harder for him, than they need be. He will find them hard enough, poor devil, before he has done with them."

And Lady Gwynne is left to ponder over what she has heard, alone.

CHAPTER IX.

THE BRIDEGROOM ELECT.

IT is not long, before Sir Lyster has hunted up the whole family of Slades, and renewed his former intimacy with them, which leads to various appointments, and invitations to dinner; and, more than once, throws Lady Gwynne, sorely against her inclination, into the society of the man, whom of all others, she is most desirous to avoid.

She has but just congratulated herself on her good fortune, when upon returning to her hotel one day, she hears that he has called during her absence, and been received by Daisy, who is eloquent on the subject of "dear Auberon's" kindness and generosity (evidenced by the production of a large wax doll, which he has brought her from the Soho Bazaar); when Sir Lyster rushes in, with an invitation to dinner at the Slades', and desires her to write an immediate acceptance for both of them.

She is very loath to do so, for she guesses from the date, that the party will be a large one; and has no hope that from such an assemblage, the bride elect will be excluded. So she pleads everything that she can think of, in favour of her being permitted to remain at home; but her husband is far more determined that she shall go.

"Why! it will be as good as an affront to refuse, without a valid reason for doing so. Don't you see that the invitation is dated a fortnight hence, only a week or two before the wedding ; and the party has doubtless been arranged with a view of introducing Miss Cameron to their friends ? Of course we must go !   You seem to think very little of your position in society, Lady Gwynne ; but I am not forgetful of mine, nor of what I owe to such old friends as the Slades. People of our standing must consent at times, to forego their private wishes, in consideration of the public good."

Sir Lyster talks as though he were the Prince of Wales, or the Duke of Cambridge, or just a little bigger and more important than either of those gentlemen ; and Lady Gwynne disputes the point no longer, but obeys his demand, and cherishes a huge contempt for his opinions.

So she foregoes her private wishes for

the public good, and is dragged to the big dinner party, feeling as though she were being led to execution; and only trusting that it will prove to be so large that the love-making she dreads to witness, may be carried on without her cognisance.

But she is not doomed to undergo that needless torture. The assembly is a very numerous one, and the son of the house is present; but the bride elect is nowhere to be seen.

Lady Gwynne soon discovers the fact, and is grateful for it. She feels somehow as though her gratitude were due to Auberon for this relief; as though it must have been through his agency, strategic or straightforward, that so important a guest has been omitted from the list of invitations.

And she is right : Auberon Slade may be weak and wilful, even wicked, but his memory is not quite so defective, nor his heart so callous, as to permit him to parade his new courtship beneath the eyes of the woman, to whom, but a few short weeks before, he had promised to be faithful until death.

He performs the multifarious duties, which, as eldest son of the house, fall to his share, with assiduity : dutifully paying court to all the old dowagers, to whom his mother directs his attention, and finally going down to dinner with twenty stone of widow, surmounted by a very red face and an undeniable wig, upon his arm. But he looks pale and worried, nevertheless ; not near so brave and gallant as when he broke that news to her, behind the curtains at the theatre ; and Lady

Gwynne is thankful, on taking her seat at the dinner-table, to find that he is divided from her by a string of guests, and a mountain of flowers, so that by no possibility can she catch, even a glimpse of, the features of his face. The temporary separation lessens her trial, which, even with the help of that alleviation, seems at times more than she can calmly bear.

It is almost worse when dinner is concluded, and the ladies are in the drawing-room, for then his mother and sisters cluster about her as the most important person there, and drive her nearly wild with descriptions of the impending ceremony : and assurances of the beauty, amiability, and grace of the future Mrs. Auberon Slade.

"Oh ! such a sweet creature, Lady Gwynne. I wish she had been here tonight, you would have been charmed with her, I am sure : and so devoted to my brother !"

"Such simplicity ! such grace ! such childlike innocence !" exclaims the mother-in-law expectant.

"Ah ! you are talking of Miss Charlotte Cameron !"—this from a sympathetic guest. "She is, indeed, all that you say. Mr. Powlett assured me yesterday that he had seldom met with a more amiable disposition."

"There is her *carte-de-visite*," interrupts the second sister, as she bears forward, one of those museums of ugliness, photograph albums. "Now Lady Gwynne shall see what she is like."

"Oh ! but that doesn't do her justice."

"Well, no picture could do that !"

"No! dear Lottie's forte lies in her colour. She is as fresh as a rose."

"Yes! I heard Auberon call her his moss rosebud the other day. Rather a pretty simile, I thought, as her hair waves naturally."

"Oh! now, Emma! that is too bad of you, telling poor Auberon's secrets; what a shame! But I am sure Lady Gwynne will not let it go any further, for Auberon is so very particular; it would vex him terribly to have it known."

Amidst some such chorus as the above, she takes up the photograph, and looks at it, and for the first moment is disposed to agree with Mr. Norris, that the original can possess neither beauty, nor talents, nor grace; for the picture is that of an ordinary-looking girl, with rather heavy features, and inclined to stoutness, sitting in a very inelegant attitude, and clad in a hideous plaid dress.

But Miss Charlotte Cameron—like many a photographic victim—is not nearly so black as she is painted, for her chief glories, which consist in reddish gold hair and a very bright complexion, are worse than lost, beneath the untender mercies of the sun.

Lady Gwynne knows nothing of this, however, or is not in a position to realise it, and can therefore only gaze silently at the representation before her, and wonder what Auberon can have found to charm him in the original.

And the interpolatory remarks of Miss Cameron's intended sisters-in-law do not help her to a solution of the mystery.

" Dear Lottie ! She looks a little sulky

there, doesn't she, Lady Gwynne? But I
am sure it is quite an error: she never
sulks."

" Oh! I have seen Lottie look just like
that when she is put out. I think it a
very good likeness; and so does Auberon,
for yesterday when Mrs. Randall remarked
that it was not flattering, he said it was
as like as two peas, which I thought very
strong."

" Well, but I don't think Lottie is
sulky. Mamma, dear, do you consider
Lottie at all sulky?"

" Oh, no, my dear; but I should say she
had a spirit of her own. She is a very
fine character."

" Ah! well! all women should have
some spirit, shouldn't they, Lady Gwynne?
And it will do Auberon good sometimes,
not to have his own way."

"Here is Auberon, so I shall tell him what you say, Emma."

"No ! don't."

"Yes, I shall !   Auberon !"

Lady Gwynne claps the pages of the album hastily together, and deposits it upon the nearest table. She would not have him see what she has been contemplating, nor hear what they have been discussing, for the world. She longs to get up, and move to another part of the drawing-room, but it is too late. Attracted by his sister's voice, he is already amongst them, looking as gloomy and dissatisfied as he was before.

"What is it, Margaret ? Did you call me ?"

"Yes ; there is treason hatching here. I want to tell you what Emma has been

saying about you and Lottie! She says
——"

. "No! don't, Margaret!"

"Be quiet, Emma! You shouldn't say such things if you don't wish to have them repeated. She says——"

But what she says, Auberon Slade is never destined to hear, for the cloud upon his brow changes to a frown, and he is already moving away from them.

"Can't you talk sense?" he exclaims, angrily. "Are there no topics of interest with which to amuse your guests, than these abominable discussions upon home affairs? When will you learn that domestic details are engrossing to none, but the parties concerned in them?"

And he walks off at once to the other end of the apartment.

The sisters, with bated breath, and looks of awe, glance comically at one another.

"There, now, Margaret; you've put him out."

"Well, it was all your fault, if I have."

"But you need not have repeated what I said of him. You know how he dislikes to be talked about."

"Ah! well! he will have forgotten it by to-morrow; and if not, we must get Lottie to coax him into good-humour again."

And so on, and so on; until Lady Gwynne's carriage is announced, and she rises wearily to bid good-night to her entertainers, and is thankful to find that the old gentleman considers it his especial duty to lead her down-stairs, and start her safely on her journey home. How grateful she is to find herself once more there.

The slow torture she undergoes in these days of uncertainty and suspense, seems to be the worst which she has yet experienced.

CHAPTER X.

A GREAT CHANGE.

SHE meets Auberon Slade on several occasions after this, for the dinner at his father's house is quickly followed by one given by themselves, at the hotel, at which Sir Lyster announces that he has taken a double box at Drury Lane Theatre for the next evening, that the whole party may enjoy the Christmas Pantomime together, and to her astonishment, Auberon pleads no previous engagement, as an excuse for declining either invitation. That he should voluntarily choose to meet her, who would at any moment have turned miles out of her way to avoid encountering him, is a marvel to Lady Gwynne; and from it, she can only draw the bitter inference, that even the sight of her has ceased to give him pain. But that he does meet her, is all that can be said for him. Auberon Slade continues to laugh, and talk as much as he used to do, even more; but he never laughs, or talks with Lady Gwynne.

To her, he addresses slow monosyllabic sentences, chiefly dictated by the exigencies of etiquette, during the delivery of which, he keeps his eyes (so unchanged in their expression, when she is not regarding them) fixed upon her face, until, perhaps by chance, she raises her own, to find that he is looking

indifferently in quite an opposite direction.

The alteration in his voice and manner,
as he turns to speak to some one else,
fills her crushed jealous heart with envy;
it appears so light and gay, so full of
interest; could she behold it when, striving
to copy his assumed impassibility, lest he
should guess the pain it causes her, she
also laughs and talks with other men,
Lady Gwynne would lose her fear that
he has forgotten what she was to him.
For then it is that his next neighbour
is surprised to find that Auberon Slade
has suddenly grown deaf and oblivious
of her company, and sits, silent and abstracted, darting angry, moody glances on
the male miscreant opposite to him, who
dares to be powerful enough to call forth
a smile upon the pale face of his hostess,

or to make the old well-remembered dimples appear about the corners of her mouth.

Then it is, may be, that Gwendoline Gwynne, led by that inexplicable sympathy which, from the first, has united her to Auberon Slade, knows by instinct that he is gazing at her; and looking up with a sudden quick glance of misery (uncontrollable because undesigned), pierces his heart deeper than a thousand reproaches could do. And in those moments, few and far between, which come and go like summer lightning, their hearts once more speak to one another, and she knows, that whatever has alienated him from her, prudence, conscience, or distrust, she is still dear to him, if only for the memory of what has been.

And thanks God for the knowledge, even whilst she admits that it would be

far better if he could lose remembrance
of it all.

Sometimes, during those painful hours
of trying to solve a mystery which is in-
soluble, she feels as though she could no
longer endure the misery of suspense;
and must go up to him, and boldly take
his hand, and say, " Auberon ! what has
divided us ? only tell me, in order that
I may help, instead of hinder you, upon
the path that duty has doubtless incited
you to take."   And had he formed no
fresh engagement, made no pretence of a
new love, she would assuredly, by her
honesty, have been led to demand an explanation of him.

But with every thought of it, with every
conviction that, considering the circumstances under which they parted, it would
be not only excusable but the right thing

to do, comes the remembrance of Charlotte Cameron, of the ordinary-looking, second-rate, inanimate being for whose affection he has seen fit to barter hers—and pride keeps her back from speaking to him.

Shall she let him imagine that she still wears the willow, which he plucked (withered) from his brow, before it had rested there a month ?

No ! she cannot ; she *will not !*

When she imagined that his heart was all her own, pride died in her breast, but a hydra-headed monster has been nurtured there upon the knowledge that he *can* take another to his arms.

Auberon !—*her* Auberon !—the husband of another woman !

Merciful powers ! take her life before the day arrives on which the act is to be accomplished.

And there is so little time—so little, little time !

Little time ! Yes ! could he not have waited ? If his heart is so cold, his love so poor and weak, his impatience to forget so strong, might he not at least have reached the goal of his desires without trampling over the still writhing carcase of her fallen hope ; of crushing utterly her feeble ray of happiness ?

Was it necessary for him to rush into marriage with a lie in his right hand ? as false to the woman he is about to wed, as to the one whom he has deserted !

But here she remembers that she sent him from her ; that she drove him forth as he had prophesied she would, comfortless and alone ; alike bereft of love and hope, left to himself and the first distraction that might happen to lie in his path.

And did she not resign him to his God; place his dear love, as well as his dear self, an offering upon the altar of their mutual Lord? And dare she regret what she has done; grudge her devotion; consider the sacrifice too great; or think she retains any claim to influence or order the actions of his future life?

She knows that she does not, that she *dares* not; and with the softer, better mood, the woman's real feelings gain the upper hand, and tears fall gently on her lap in pity for—not in condemnation of—the man who will ever hold the first place in her heart.

So that the explanation never comes, although a desire for it continues very strong; and Lady Gwynne associates with Auberon Slade as if she knew no more of him than of his sisters; and, with his aid, unasked, but given, has battled successfully hitherto (notwithstanding Sir Lyster's vigorous efforts to bring about an opposite result) against the danger and the dread, which she cannot overcome, of encountering Miss Charlotte Cameron.

If at this period my story seems to repeat itself, and runs the risk of wearying its readers by dwelling too often, and too long, upon the thoughts and feelings of my heroine, it is because her mind has become a constant repetition of questions that are never answered, but fall back from the voiceless air upon her heart, to gnaw it night and day, and leave it always unsatisfied and restless.

She cannot arrive at a decision concerning Auberon Slade; his acquaintance find no difficulty in giving a name to his behaviour, but her love will not permit her to

do so. In her mind, which revels in torturing itself, he is " everything by turns,
and nothing long."

One hour she feels sure that he is acting
prudently, the next, that he has cruelly
deceived her ; in the morning believes she is
still loved, by nightfall is certain he has quite
forgotten. The evening may find her resting contentedly in the belief that God has
ordered all for the best, whilst noon will see
her on her knees in a paroxysm of despair,
vainly demanding why such things are.

She is very meek and gentle at this
time with her husband, for she is subdued
by all that she has gone through, and
anxious in some measure to atone to him
for the unpremeditated infidelity into which
each hour betrays her. But on one point
she is very firm, and unfortunately it is a
point which is considered by Sir Lyster an

important one—she obstinately refuses to accept the invitation which has been sent her, to appear at the wedding of Auberon Slade and Charlotte Cameron. Not at the instigation of the bridegroom - elect, of that she is well aware ; it has issued straight from the hand of his mother and sisters ; but whoever may desire her presence, she refuses to accede to the request. She has suffered sufficiently (so she tells herself), without the endurance of this last agony, which is no part of the sacrifice that Heaven has marked out for her.

Sir Lyster is more than vexed at his wife's refusal, he is excessively angry ; for he attributes her firmness entirely to caprice, or a malicious desire to annoy him through the medium of his friends.

She has plenty of time, and dresses, and money ! what the devil should prevent her from devoting a single morning to gracing the wedding breakfast of the Slades ? For that Lady Gwynne does grace any scene in which she chooses to appear, Sir Lyster is not quite such a fool, nor so tired of her, as to attempt to deny.

But he has conceived a violent admiration for Miss Charlotte Cameron, and not only desires that his wife should pay her the compliment of appearing interested in her marriage ceremony, but make her a suitable present, in both their names, on the occasion.

Something handsome, and worthy of the donors, he says ostentatiously (it is long since he has presented anything " hand- some " to either Daisy or her mother), a bracelet, or set of brooch and earrings —emeralds will suit Miss Cameron's com plexion better than any other stones—and

Lady Gwynne had better go to Hunt and Roskell's, and choose it herself.

But Lady Gwynne utterly refuses to do so. Miss Cameron, from all accounts, has plenty of rich friends to make her presents, and she does not consider that either she or the Slades have any claim upon them.

"If you are determined to give her something, Lyster, and Auberon Slade will permit his wife to accept a gift from you, you must do it on your own account. I decline to have anything to do with the matter."

"Damn it, madam! do you suppose I shall allow you to fly in my face in this manner?"

"You cannot force me to break through the rules of society, because you have taken a fancy to a pretty face! Nor to appear at a ceremony for which I have no taste. I hate weddings and wedding breakfasts, and everything connected with them."

"So do I—in retrospection."

"You know that I am not usually disobedient to you, Lyster. But in this case I must be firm. My presence or absence can make no difference to the breakfast-party, nor to your appearance at it; and as for the present, I am sure that no one would be more astonished than Miss Cameron herself, at receiving a bracelet from a person to whom she is utterly unknown!"

"Very well! very well! have your own way! You'll repent of it before the day is out—that's all I can tell you."

"If I do, it will not be my fault! I cannot act differently!"

"*I* shall be at the wedding, anyway—I suppose you have no objection to that?"

" Oh, Lyster ! how could I have ?   I am sure that your presence will quite atone for my absence. You are a much more important personage than I am. And they all know that poor Daisy is laid upon her back," she answers with alacrity, thankful to think she has got over her difficulty with so much ease.

" Very well !   That will be the day after to-morrow, and we shall go back to Felton the same afternoon."

" The same afternoon !" she falters.

She has imagined they are to remain in London for a month longer at the very least; for although Dr. Aberystwith has pronounced his opinion concerning Daisy's spine, the child is still under his care, and rigidly pursuing the treatment he recommends ; and Lady Gwynne knows that she will lose considerably by being sent back so soon to Dr. Stewart and the country.

" The same afternoon, Lyster,—how can we? Dr. Aberystwith said only yesterday that Daisy must continue the chemical baths for at least three weeks longer, before he will be able to judge what effect they are likely to produce, or to decide upon any plan for her future treatment."

" That's nothing to me," returns Sir Lyster, as though his wife had been talking of the ailments of a favourite dog. " I'm sick of town, and I don't intend to remain in it an hour after Slade has gone. I want to find myself back at Felton, and where I am, you must be. You packed up your traps in less than two days to come here, so you will have no difficulty in being ready at the proper time. Now, don't

14—2

forget ! we go home by the four o'clock
train on Thursday."

"But, Lyster, do consider the child ! I
wouldn't care for myself (you know I would
not.) I had no desire to visit London, and
I shall be very glad to leave it again ; but
for Daisy's sake—it is so very important ;
Dr. Aberystwith says that the comfort of
her whole life, may depend upon the strict-
ness with which we carry out the treatment of the first few months !"

She might as well appeal to the table or
the chair, or any other of the inanimate
articles by which she is surrounded ; for
she has baulked and thwarted Sir Lyster,
and he will carry out his noble revenge.
She has refused to put on that fawn-
coloured silk and Brussels-lace bonnet which
he knows she has amongst her stock of
clothing, and, replete with smiles of con-

gratulation, appear at Auberon Slade's wedding, to wish him as much joy in his married life as she has found in hers ; and when an English moral slave refuses to obey, she must be taught that there is such a thing as a bowstring for the inclination, and a bastinado for the heart. And should that heart be bound up in the welfare of another, and a still more defenceless nature than her own, what better means to make it wince, than when the blow falls second-hand ?

"I don't care a hang for old Aberystwith or any other confounded humbug! The child is mine,.and I choose that she shall return to Felton ; and there's no law in England to prevent a father doing as he wills with his own."

"I know there is not," she replies sadly ; "for the laws of this world are woefully defective in the narrow margin that they leave for possibilities ; but there is a law of God, Lyster (the God who regards both you and me at this present moment, and judges between us), that is capable of outwitting all the laws of England, if He will it so."

He makes no answer to her speech, except by setting a couple of chairs before her, and after apologising for the rudeness of her pulpit and the paucity of her congregation, requesting that she will at once continue the sermon she has so successfully commenced.

"I am not an advocate for week-day services, as you are perhaps aware," he goes on maliciously ; "but on this occasion, and in consideration of the intense interest I take in your subject, I waive my natural objections."

His irony silences her.

" I can say no more, Lyster.   I suppose it must be as you desire.   If you will not postpone our departure for Daisy's sake, I know you will not do it for mine."

The sound of tears is in her lowered voice, but it does not soften him.

" Oh ! you have come to your senses, have you—very well ! then—we understand each other !   Thursday—at four o'clock !   And if old Aberystwith makes any demur upon the subject, you may tell him, with my compliments, to go to the devil."

Saying which, Sir Lyster Gwynne leaves the apartment, without another glance at his insulted wife.

She cannot cry ; she almost wishes that she could, but her tears seem dried up in their sources, and suffering now only makes her brow beat, and sighs well up thickly from her bosom.

And she has still Daisy to think for, and to prepare for the coming change; and whilst there is another dependant on herself for comfort or support, Lady Gwynne (as Mr. Lawrence told her), will neither faint nor fail.

The wedding-day arrives, a gloomy, lowering day in February, with unborn snow in the leaden-coloured sky, and a bitter north wind sweeping round the corners of the streets; a most unfavourable day (so Dr. Aberystwith says) to move his patient to the country. Yet Sir Lyster's decree remains unchanged, and the bill is paid and the boxes packed, and every preparation made for their departure; and Lady Gwynne sits in the cheerless drawing-room, watching for her husband's entrance, and wondering if he can have forgotten at what hour he ordered them to be ready to start. He quitted the hotel before eleven, and it is past three, and he has not returned. Surely the wedding break-fast cannot be prolonged till now.

The hours have passed but wearily to Lady Gwynne, as may be well imagined; but, for her child's sake, she has borne up bravely against what she knows to be inevitable, and marvellously evinced the possession of that patience for which she has so often prayed.

And now it must be over, and the die of Auberon Slade's destiny irrevocably cast. Henceforward he can be nothing to her, excepting in her prayers. She sits quietly amongst the travelling cases, and bundles of wraps and umbrellas, vainly striving to pierce the future of his fate

and hers, yet interrupting the little heart-
broken petitions for his happiness, that rise
continuously from her labouring breast,
to give a freshly-thought-of order, or im-
press an old direction, so that no one
guesses, from the calmness with which she
goes through her duty, that with every
moment numbered by the clock, hope re-
cedes further from her, and desolation
becomes more sure.

Yet so are half the tragedies of this
deceptive world played out.

"Mamma, darling! it is four o'clock;
how can we go to Felton to-day? And
I am so tired, do put me back to
bed."

The childish complaint rouses Lady
Gwynne from her reverie more effectually
than anything else could have done, and
she starts to find that Daisy's informa-

tion is indeed correct, and the time fixed
for their departure, past.

How is she to act; what next to do?
There is no other train to Felton until ten
at night, and surely Sir Lyster will
never dream of exposing the little invalid
at such an hour. Besides, the child is
already fretful, and wearied out with the
protracted waiting, and upon further consideration the mother determines to brave
everything, even her husband's anger,
sooner than entail a longer trial on her
weakened frame. So Daisy is put back
to bed, as she desires, and made happy
with the assurance that she may lie there,
without any fear of being disturbed again
until the following day; whilst Lady
Gwynne, after laying aside her bonnet
and shawl, returns to the sitting-room
to resume the watch that has been in-

terrupted by the attendance on her child.

She is just a little nervous now of encountering Sir Lyster; for she knows how violent and unreasonable he can be, and is not sure whether he will excuse her conduct in having waited for his return, nor say that she should have proceeded to Felton without him.

But she has acted as she believed he desired her to do; and tries to hope, that, this time at least, he will say she has been right.

Yet she changes colour with every step that sounds upon the stairs, and heaves a sigh of relief as it passes her apartment, and five, six, seven o'clock come and go, and Sir Lyster is still absent.

Then she is really frightened—not that he has come to any harm (it is only hearts that love, that fret themselves to death with such sweet, needless worries), but that finding himself late, he has gone straight to the railway station (assuming he will meet her there), and thence to Felton; and will break all the vials of his wrath on her devoted head when next they meet.

She thinks of sending some one to the Slades' to ask if he has left the house, and at what time, and rings the bell with that intention; but when it is responded to, something in the servant's manner tells her that news has been received.

"Is Sir Lyster home?" she demands eagerly.

"No, my lady;—but—but—Mr. Slade (the old gentleman, my lady) would be glad to speak with you for a few minutes."

"Show him up at once," she answers, and stands upon her feet until the old man's tardy steps have reached the door.

"What is it, Mr. Slade? Please tell me at once—I cannot bear suspense."

The solemn expression of his face has already informed her that bad news (or what the world will call "bad" news) is coming, and her words are uttered in a tone of so much excitement, that Mr. Slade considers it necessary to use a double amount of caution and prosiness in breaking the intelligence he has brought her.

"My dear Lady Gwynne," he commences slowly, "I am indeed grieved to be the bearer of sad news to you; but I trust that you will call all your powers of fortitude to bear upon——"

She turns, if anything, paler than

she has turned before, and grasps the back of the chair by which she stands.

"Mr. Slade! I conjure you in God's name to be brief. Is it—is it my husband—or—or—any one else?"

"I regret to say it is indeed Sir Lyster, of whom I come to speak to you. He——"

"Is he only injured, or—or—*dead?*"

Mr. Slade bows his head—

"*Dead*—dead! How? When?"

"Oh! my dear lady! be strong—be strong!"

"I *am* strong! When did it happen?"

"Immediately after our young couple left us for their tour."

"And how?"

"Very suddenly! It was an awful shock to us as you may imagine—we had the best attendance, at once upon the spot.

I believe the doctors consider it was apo-
plexy."

*   *   *   *   *   *

There is complete silence in the gloomy
room ; the old man, with his eyes cast
upon the ground, stands by the table ;
the woman still grasps the back of the
friendly chair.

"Lady Gwynne! for the sake of your
child ; of those still left ; I pray you——"

"Mr. Slade! will you do me one great
kindness?   Leave me to myself."

*   *   *   *   *   *

So he leaves her, to try and realise
her great deliverance, and her great
despair.

CHAPTER XI.

WIDOWHOOD.

HER *great deliverance!* I wonder if the expression will strike harshly on the ear of any one who may read these pages!

Did they, instead of recording a real life, as Nature made, and God transformed it, treat of the sorrows of a mere conventional heroine, they might tell how the announcement of her husband's sudden death is followed, on the part of Lady Gwynne, by a burst of violent sorrow for his loss, and lamentation for her past behaviour to him.

But it is not the case : why, it would be impossible to say, unless, indeed, because it is not natural, and Gwendoline Gwynne is essentially so.

She has sinned against Heaven and against earth ; she has followed the leading of her own impulses, and bitterly repented the fatal issue into which they so nearly betrayed her—she is quite aware of that. But—she has lived the joyless, cheerless life of a prisoner in captivity, linked to a man without love, or sympathy, or consideration ; and God has seen fit to break her bonds, and she has too much honesty to delude herself into the belief that she is not thankful.

To say that the news of so sudden a deliverance is not a shock to her, would be to write her down unwomanly, and unchristian ; for the mere knowledge that her husband has been called away without a moment for repentance is sufficient to appal her. Oh, how awful it is to think over his last words, his last acts, and to remember that he has passed into the Hands of Judgment!

Her first thought upon receiving the intelligence is a thanksgiving, that through all her troubles she has never been tempted to wish for his decease; her first impulse, a great desire to fall upon her knees and intercede with God for mercy on his soul. And so, as soon as Mr. Slade has left her side, she does; and offers up her prayer, not only for the dead, but for herself, that, left to her own guidance, she may be enabled to lead a better and a holier life, and rear her child to do the same.

And if with this petition there comes another, mingled with far bitterer tears, that plead for resignation to the Will that has permitted her to miss, as it were by a hair's breadth, the happiness for which she was willing to give up so much, who shall blame her?

Not you, Madam! who cover your skirts with crape, and use envelopes bordered an inch deep in woe, for a husband whom you worried to the grave; nor you, who, still residing beneath the protection of yours, and turning up your nose in virtuous indignation at the poor painted wretches who pass you in the streets, yet keep your assignations, and your generous friends, and your mysterious presents, wherewith to mystify your more innocent, or ignorant acquaintance!

The world is a great universal humbug, that outwits itself, and makes it easy to guess who deserves the greatest censure, by her who passes it the most readily.

The shock to Lady Gwynne is an undoubted fact, for no woman ever less expected to be left a widow than herself. Sir Lyster! so strong, so hale, so hearty! with his florid complexion, stalwart arm, loud voice, and capabilities of appetite— whoever would have dreamt that he would have been cut off, without a moment's warning, like an infant of an hour old? His wife has overlooked the thick coarse throat, plethoric temperament, and unrestrained desires, which might have warned a more experienced eye, that when the citadel gave in, it would be suddenly. And some such suspicion may have struck the man himself, which would account for his unreasonable dislike to everything that was connected with illness or its cure, and intolerant of the least exhibition of weakness in another.

Well! it is over—and the fears, the foibles, and the sins of Lyster Gwynne will alike be buried with him in the grave! She learns many more particulars of his behaviour on that last day afterwards; how he was the heartiest and the jolliest at the wedding breakfast, giving the health of the bride and the bridegroom in a speech which excited the laughter and the admiration of all present, and been amongst the foremost to throw satin slippers after the carriage in which they drove away.

How, on re-entering the house, he expressed a wish for a cigar, and accompanied Mr. Slade and some of his guests to a room which they had set apart for smoking, where, by his anecdotes and *bon-mots*, he had kept the whole company in a roar, and not risen to return to his hotel until the clock had long struck five.

And finally—how, whilst even in the act of reaching for his hat and great coat in the hall, he had staggered forward, and then back, and finally fallen prostrate on the floor, where life was pronounced to be extinct, even though five minutes did not elapse between his seizure and the arrival of professional assistance.

She listens to these details calmly, so calmly, indeed, that old Mrs. Slade prophesies that when Lady Gwynne does give way, the reaction will be terrible—little dreaming, good old soul, that throughout her prosy and oft-repeated narrative, her passive listener has been trying to unravel, not the reason why God has taken the dead man from her, but that old mystery which tortured her brain before, and has returned with tenfold force upon it now—why He ever permitted her to meet Auberon Slade, or, so permitting, turned the current of events out of their natural course, in order to make life still more perplexing to her than it was before !

She leaves her child in London, under the care of Dr. Aberystwith and an able nurse, and accompanies her husband's body down to Felton Hall, and watches by it faithfully, until the last offices of friendship and religion are performed, and it is consigned to the mausoleum of his forefathers.

And then, for the first time, Lady Gwynne seems to have leisure to pause, and plan the purpose of her future life.

She cannot live at Felton, nor indeed anywhere in the same degree of luxury that she has done hitherto.

As Sir Lyster leaves no male heir in the direct line, the Hall, together with the Welsh estates, and certain property in other parts of England, go, with the title, to his cousin, Captain, now Sir Richard Gwynne, who has spent all his life in India, and scarcely knows the old place by sight.

The late baronet has made all the provision that he can for his wife and daughter, by settling private property to the amount of eight hundred a-year upon the former, and an old country place called "The Orchard House," situated in the village of Warmouth, Dorsetshire, and producing a rental of some eighty pounds a-year, upon the latter; a very sorry pittance, so Mr. Lawrence considers it; but the widow is of a totally different opinion.

" Eight hundred and eighty a-year, Mr. Lawrence, and only for Daisy and myself.

Oh, I think it is ample. I shall take a snug little house, somewhere in Kensington or Brompton, and keep a couple of servants, and we shall be as happy as the day is long."

" Live in London ! Is that really your intention ?"

His thoughts are expressed in his face, and Lady Gwynne guesses them, and blushes like a rose.

He is thinking that she ought not to take up her residence in the same place as Auberon Slade.

" Why not ? Where would you have me go to ?"

But she puts the question in a subdued voice, and very much with the manner of a child that knows beforehand what the answer it receives, will be.

" Not to London, decidedly. The seaside would be twice as advantageous to Daisy."

"But Dr. Aberystwith ! She is under his care."

" She will not be so always. However, ask his advice upon the subject. I am quite sure he will agree with me, that for a weakly child, the country or sea air is preferable to that of town."

There is silence between them for a few moments, which he breaks with the sudden query :

" Why not reside at the Orchard House itself ?"

" The Orchard House ? Why, I thought it was a rickety, tumble-down old place, not fit for anyone ?"

" How do you expect to get eighty pounds a-year for it, if it is in that con-dition ?" he rejoins, laughing. " I know the last time I saw it I thought it a most charming retreat."

"Do you know Warmouth, then?"

"I know Barnes, the curate there, very well, and I believe it is a place that would suit you in every respect. Major and Mrs. Ferrars had the Orchard House when I passed through there last summer, but I believe it was only for a short term, or their lease was nearly expired, for I remember Barnes lamenting over their probable departure. He would be charmed to get you for a parishioner."

But she is still unwilling to entertain the thought; it seems such a long distance to put between herself and all her friends : such an unnecessary aggravation of her lonely and desolate condition.

"But is it not rather enervating?" she suggests, next.

"I think not. Warmouth is mild, like all the Dorsetshire coast ; but the Orchard House stands on a hill, and overlooks the village. And then it is by the sea, which I should consider a great thing for Daisy."

"But her education !"

"There are towns close at hand, from which you could get masters. And under any circumstances now, her studies must be conducted at home."

"Eight hundred will certainly go further in the country than it would in London," she answers, thoughtfully.

"Dear Lady Gwynne ! it is not a question of money, it is one of expediency ; nay, more of right. I daresay you think, now circumstances are so altered, that, come what may, you are perfectly secure ;

but you are very much mistaken. 'The heart is deceitful above all things, and desperately wicked;' never more so than when, under the guise of security, it lures us on to our destruction."

"Oh! Mr. Lawrence! you do not think —you cannot imagine——"

"I think nothing of you, dear friend, but what is perfectly good, and true, and pure. So much so, that I do not believe you will even put yourself in the way of temptation when it is once pointed out to you. And that is why, in urging you to take up your residence at the Orchard House, or some other country place, I feel confident that eventually you will follow my advice."

"But if I am not to live in town," she answers, unconsciously assenting to his words, "I should so much have liked to be near you."

"And I should have had the greatest pleasure in feeling you were my neighbour, Lady Gwynne; but I do not counsel it, for two reasons. One is, that you would not find it pleasant to occupy a secondary position where you have held the first: and the other, that this place, and the associations linked to it, are not good for you. You had much better seek new scenes and new faces, and leave the past to bury itself."

"Your medicine is always so bitter," she says, with a melancholy smile.

"But it cures, my child, it cures. I believe you are the better for it, even now."

"I feel the safer," she whispers, with

her hand in his; and from that hour makes up her mind, that if all things agree to render the plan feasible, she will become the mistress in reality, as well as name, of the Orchard House.

CHAPTER XII.

THE ORCHARD HOUSE.

BUILT of grey stone in the fashion of a century ago, and backed by timber that was planted at the time that it was built, the Orchard House looks proudly down from the summit of the hill on which it stands, upon the more modern edifices of Warmouth.

It is a charming, old-fashioned place, though not very large, with Gothic windows, and a heavy, iron-bound door; and the kitchen and flower-gardens by which it is surrounded, are enclosed by a high wall, which gives it the appearance of a nunnery.

Indeed, it is generally supposed in Warmouth that the Orchard House was once dedicated to conventual purposes ; for a tiny chapel, now the exclusive property of Mr. Barnes, and the orthodox services of which (to the extreme disgust of the vicar) have emptied the principal pews in the parish church, stands almost within its grounds, and is embowered by trees and shrubs that formed a part of the convent garden.

A large orchard, as its modern name im‧plies, lies at the side of the house, whilst the green hill in front slopes down to a peaceful valley, spread over by rich fields ; beyond which the eye rests upon the village of Warmouth, and the rough dancing waves, divided from it only by the green cliffs and shelving rocky beach.

Lady Gwynne, in virtue of her resolution, goes down to see this place, and though the season is unfavourable and the trees are bare, falls in love with it at once.

There is an air of peace and quiet pervading the old Orchard House, that appeals very powerfully to her aching heart, weary of hoping and longing, and being disappointed, and makes her feel as though, once settled here with Daisy, she might even outgrow her present trouble, and learn to lead a simple and comfortable life. She delights in the appearance of the low-roofed, wainscoted apartments; the quaintly designed bed-rooms, that lead into each other by little flights of steps; the prim old-fashioned parlours; the straight narrow paths of the flower garden; and the old trees and standard bushes, that have bloomed and blossomed there for years.

16--2

The house is empty, for the last tenants only held it for a year, and it is supposed to be furnished, although the dull, sober coloured carpets and curtains, and the uncomfortable looking beds and chairs, cause Lady Gwynne alternately to shudder and to smile. But all that will soon be rectified, for she has some few possessions of her own, and her income, moderate though it may be, is sufficient to supply her and her child with all the necessaries of life. So that she makes light of every obstacle, and goes through the rooms, and grounds, and stables, with such a cheerful countenance, and springing step, that the old gardener and his wife, who have been left in charge, and have been somewhat awed in prospect of a visit of inspection from the owner of the property, agree in the conclusion, that she is the " bonniest widow as ever they clapped eyes on, and no more notion of sorrow in her face, than if she were a baby."

Ah! simple hearts! that have never known worse care themselves, than what has been occasioned by a scarcity of bread or fuel, or a parting with Joe and Nancy on their first desertion of the home nest, to go to service or to sea; what would they think, could they be made to understand the tempests that have racked this woman's soul!

Can it be, that education and refinement, and the march of intellect, instead of rendering us stronger, make us less capable of bearing our griefs well; or do nerves and frame keep pace together, and have the rough skin and the rough mind, no capability of suffering in measure with ourselves?

For it is undoubtedly true that, with the exception of a very few cases, the labouring poor do not suffer the mental anguish that we do ; they make a great noise over trouble when it comes, but they have neither the faculty of bearing it silently, nor long.

Could the old gardener and his wife, alluded to, be told that this lady, who looks so young to them, whose buoyant step they follow with admiration, and whose eye they see brighten, as it lights upon each fresh evidence that her future home will be a pleasant one, carries a broken heart beneath her temporary smiles, they would not believe it!   What she, who notwithstanding her deep mourning garb, and melancholy looking widow's cap, speaks so pleasantly and in such a gentle voice ; who even stops to notice the old purblind, useless watchdog, and assures them it shall remain a pensioner upon the bounty of the Orchard House ; who seems to take so keen an interest in all the news of Warmouth they garrulously communicate to her; and best of all the rest, has promised to retain their services about the garden! She, the pretty creature, with a broken heart! (whatever that may be) ; "faith! and she looks more ready for another bridegroom ; and it's what they'll hope to see her with, before they die, into the bargain ; bless her sweet eyes!" Silly old man and woman! prating of things you do not understand. Could the dark cushions of the railway carriage, in which she travels back to London, lonely and desolate, tell tales, they would record the history of a storm of tears that wetted through their thick material, and sighs, that burst reluctant from her labouring bosom, as devils cast out by the finger of their Lord.

To be planning a new life, and arranging a new home, without any thought of, any reference to *him*, except the miserable purpose of placing a barrier for ever between their future intercourse, is agony to Lady Gwynne ; but an agony which her religion and her pride will overcome.   For though she bears no enmity to Auberon Slade,— though long ago she has forgiven him the slight he has cast upon her love, and even persuaded herself, that in acting as he has done, he has acted for the best,—there is no pleasure to her in the thought of him, or mention of his name, and she believes there never can be so again.   She has but one fierce longing left predominant in her, the desire to *forget !*

Oh !   If she could but forget ; forget he ever met her ; ever loved her ; ever told her that he loved ; so that she might recon- cile his behaviour with honour, consistency and truth ; and whatever her own pain, rest on the assurance of his present happiness with comfort.　But that is impracticable to her, as it is impracticable to all who sink their hopes upon a bankrupt faith!　Many may court, but it is few who win oblivion. Yet shall her memory bring her more peace than his forgetfulness to him!

The opinion of Dr. Aberystwith coinciding with that of Mr. Lawrence, Lady Gwynne finally determines to take up her residence at Warmouth, and the natives are delighted at the prospect.　For though the Orchard House has always been considered a species of dower-house of the family of Gwynne; and under that supposition been religiously bequeathed from widow to widow, or to spinster daughter, the owners have never seen fit to occupy the place within the memory of man; and the advent of a real Lady Gwynne to take up her permanent abode amongst them is an event of no small importance to the inhabitants of Warmouth.

Speculations as to the number of servants, and horses and carriages, the baronet's widow will keep, run high amongst them; and the youthful part of the population indulge their wayward fancies, with visions of dinner and dancing parties, to be given at the Orchard House, and young men visitors, riveted to the spot for ever by the attraction of their charms.

Great, therefore, is the universal disappointment when the modest possessions of Lady Gwynne pass through the village; and the announcement is made public, through the agency of Mr. Barnes, that their new neighbour is little better than a nurse to her invalid child, and does not intend either to receive or visit, in the sense they expected her to do.

It is true that the reports of the few who venture to leave their cards at the

Orchard House, are all in favour of the young widow's looks and courteous demeanour, and that those who meet her accidentally upon the beach, or in the village, are rapturous in praise of the pensive beauty of her expression, or her tender smile; but the fact only renders the herd more eager to gain admittance to her society, whilst each day convinces them that the ambition is hopeless; Lady Gwynne seems determined to live for no one but her child.

Meanwhile (and quite unconscious of the comments her reticent behaviour is exciting), she feels more cheerful than she expected to do, for it is such a novel interest to be getting her house in order, and making every arrangement possible for Daisy's comfort.

She has brought a governess with her

from London, a young cheerful woman
with a sunny disposition, who will not
press the little invalid's brain too hard,
nor be absent from her side when her
mother is compelled to be away. So that
Lady Gwynne is at liberty to superintend
the disposition of her household treasures,
or the planning of her summer garden,
without feeling anxious on her little girl's
account ; and the bustle and consequent
exertion bring a faint colour back into
her faded cheeks, and do her good.

April is now close at hand, and in the
pleasure of tending the spring flowers
that appear in every direction, of cherish-
ing sundry broods of ducks and chickens,
and investing in a low chaise and charming
dapple-grey pony, Lady Gwynne is quite
oblivious of the fact that she is not
acquainted with half the people in War-

mouth, and finds an occasional visit from Mr. Barnes, or some of the principal county families, quite sufficient society for her contentment.

The climate is much milder in Warmouth than it used to be at Felton, and Daisy is already able to get out of doors in a reclining carriage drawn by the same fat donkey who brings up the salt water each morning for her bath, and seems to grow stronger every day, from the exercise and change of air.

And then Lady Gwynne is delighted to find that Mr. Barnes loves to see flowers on the altar of his little sanctuary, and entrusts its daily decoration to her hands, so that the green-houses acquire a fresh interest in her eyes, and she immediately devotes a large bed in the kitchen-garden to the exclusive cultivation of " immortelles."

And Sir Richard Gwynne (who appears to be a most kind-hearted and considerate young man, and desirous that the widow shall strip her late husband's property of half its belongings if it pleases her), sends her down all the pictures, and the *objets d'art* from her own sitting room (the very room, as she recalls with a quick shudder, which Auberon used to occupy whilst on his visit there), and a couple of graceful, silky, bright-eyed setters of the glorious Felton breed (for which she has expressed a fugitive desire), so that she is surrounded by objects of interest, and feels already as though she were once more *at home.*

And Emily Musgrave (who, notwithstanding the airs and graces she plays off upon the other sex, is a very natural warm-hearted girl when with her own) comes down to stay with her, and they drive about the country, and explore the villages together, and form intimate acquaintance with all the needy paupers within a circuit of five miles, by which means Lady Gwynne soon discovers, that where the appetites are so good, and the family so large, there will not be much trouble in deciding what to do with the overplus of an income of eight hundred pounds a year !

So then she is peaceful—contented—satisfied—with the care of a small country house ; the services of three maid-servants, and the companionship of an ailing child, a governess, and occasionally of a stray friend!

She would not have this new life altered, if she could, nor exchanged for the old troubles, fast receding in the background ! So she writes to Mr. Lawrence !

Does it then follow that Lady Gwynne is happy—that she has forgotten?—God of Heaven! answer for her!

Since the day on which that double tragedy was enacted, Sir Lyster's sudden death, and (to her) the far more appalling circumstance of Auberon Slade's marriage, she has never heard, nor striven to hear, one word of news of him or his bride. At the one ceremonious visit of condolence paid her by the Slades, both parties were too well bred to introduce any subject so opposite to the purpose for which they had met, as the mention of a wedding,—so that a decent silence had been rigidly maintained between them on that topic, and all she knows about him with certainty is, that he is lost to her, and it is her interest as well as duty, to steel her heart against all influences but such as are connected with the present. She tries to think of Auberon Slade now, as of one who loved her, but who died before Heaven granted her the opportunity to reward his love. She *cannot* think of him as the husband of Charlotte Cameron; it is too impossible, too strange to her, to reconcile the present with the past.

To try and fancy him, who seemed so earnest, so devoted, so despairing in her cause, calmly subsided into the nothingness of domestic life, is to call up a picture of weakness and frailty and untruth, which her true faith forbids that she should couple with the thought of him who still reigns paramount in her deserted breast.

So let her put the thought away, and never think of him, except it be when she kneels down alone, to pray that God may bless—

> "——Thy lamp to oil, thy cup to wine,
> Thy hearth to joy, thy hand to an equal touch
> Of loyal troth——"

Yet even whilst she prays—hoping, Heaven witnesses, that her prayer may be accepted—she knows, that for the fickle and the untrue, prosperity and joy will never come ; for he who has no strength to bear, has no strength to endure ; and without patience and without endurance, life's blossoms drop, one by one, withered from our hands.

Yet she prays—she would not think her prayers were uttered, unless *his* name were blended with them. She would repeat it, she *has* repeated it, when too wearied by the day's toil, or pleasures, or distresses, to pray for herself ; and even culls some joy from the simple belief that if her earnest and continual petitions cannot ward trouble from his door, they will, at least, enable him to bear it better.

But that she shall ever meet him again, associate with him, know him as a friend, Gwendoline Gwynne does not believe possible, neither does she desire it. He has destroyed all prospect of pleasure in their future intercourse ; for to see and watch him in the various phases of his domestic life, could only prove deep pain to her, and impose a forced and unnatural restraint which she does not feel strong enough to undergo. So she thinks of him, as we value the memory of one whom we have known in years long past, and look forward to encountering in Heaven ; but she never permits herself to dwell upon the memory of all that he has been to her, nor to believe that they can ever meet except as mere acquaintances. And if a lurking devil in her heart brings back at times, against her better will, the remembrance of hot words and burning kisses, and passionate, soul-thrilling looks, she rushes to her farm-yard, or her garden ; takes up a hoe, or feeds the ducks and chickens at wrong times, or calls off the setters from their midday meal, to scamper down the hill, and through the village, or anywhere that leads in a contrary direction to her own mad thoughts. And the people wonder to see her walk so fast, and whisper to each other that Lady Gwynne cannot be so delicate as she appears to be, and the doctor loves to make her out; whilst she pelts by their cottages, unheeding of their censures, and does not return until she has exhausted her slight stock of strength, and is unfit for anything but to lie down upon the sofa for the rest of the evening, and be made much of by Emily Musgrave and Miss Ward.

CHAPTER XIII.

RUN TO EARTH.

"LO! the winter is past, the rain is over and gone; the flowers appear on the earth; the time for the singing of birds is come"——to speak in more modern, but less poetical language, summer has arrived, and Lady Gwynne, with her black dress looped far above the ground, a broad-brimmed hat upon her head, and a huge pair of gardening gloves upon her dainty hands, is energetically helping old Reuben the gardener, to weed the flower beds.

She does not play at work, this delicate-looking creature, with her fair, faintly-coloured face, and blue veined fingers; but goes at it with a will, stooping over the flowers as though she had been used to stooping all her life, and filling her wooden " trug " (which a rough country lad is waiting to empty as soon as filled) in half the time that her stiff-backed old retainer takes to complete the same task.

On the lawn in front of the house, which, though small, can boast of two or three shady trees, lies Daisy in her invalid carriage, which can be transformed into a garden chair at will; it is the hour before their early dinner, a time always given up to Miss Ward for her own devices; but the child, though helpless and alone, looks perfectly content, as she alternately watches her mother's graceful movements, listens to old Reuben's fragmentary gossip, or returns to the enjoyment of her latest story book.

"Now, Reuben! we really must not talk so much," cries Lady Gwynne, who occasionally finds it very needful to check the loquacity of her companion; "you say yourself that these beds must be finished to-day, and I am sure I should be quite ashamed if anyone were to come in, and catch us in such a condition—they're quite disgraceful."

Reuben removes his hat, scratches his head, and regards the weed-grown parterre thoughtfully.

"Well, to be sure, they have got a bit ahead of us, my lady; but then, you see, there was such a mort to be done with the kitchen stuff last week, and two pair of hands is but two pair of hands after all, my lady, be they ?"

" Not a bit of it, Reuben," is the cheerful answer ; " two such hands as yours and mine, are equal to a dozen ordinary ones. But we talk too much, Reuben ! it's a fact, though a melancholy one ! But now, if you'll make a resolution to finish your flower-bed before the first dinner-bell rings, I'll do the same by mine. What time is it, Daisy ?"

" Half-past twelve, mamma."

" Oh ! come ! that's famous, we have an whole hour before us. The ' trug ' is ready, Jack ; make haste and empty it, and Reuben's will be full by the time you come back."

The old gardener looks at his " trug " which contains about a dozen roots and half-a-dozen stones, and chuckles over her ladyship's idea as though it were the best joke in the world.

" Now, bless your heart, my dear lady, I'm not so young as you are ; I wish I was —I wish I was.   It's the young that have the enjoyment of this world, as everybody knows."

" Do you think so, Reuben ?" with a sigh.   " I don't know.   Life's burthen appears to me to be pretty equally apportioned to us all.   How is the old wife's rheumatism this morning ?"

" Well, it's wonderfully the better, my lady, for the embrocation you sent her ; and she eat all the supper as Miss Ward had the goodness to bring last night. Oh, it's folks like yourself as makes life tolerable to the poor !   Have you heard that we're to have new gentlefolk in the village, my lady ?"

" No, Reuben. I've heard nothing about it," replies Lady Gwynne, as she returns to her employment. " What are their names ?"

" I didn't rightly catch the name, my lady ; indeed I can't say, as Bob Kent, who told me of it, had heard the name himself ; but it's Fernside as they're looking after, the house on the right hand side as you drives into Warmouth."

" Oh, I know !" with sudden interest. " That pretty place that stands in a little kind of park, with large iron gates and a sunk fence on the road-side ; the house that Mr. Barnes tells me General Clifford lived in last year."

" That's the place, my lady ; though as to its being so pretty, I don't know. I don't hold out to be any judge myself, but to my mind the Orchard House is the prettiest place about here by a good bit, and I said so, long before you came to live in it."

" Fernside," she continues musingly, and apparently without having paid any attention to the old gardener's last words, " I wonder who can have taken Fernside ! It is too lonely and retired to suit most tastes. Do you know whether it is let furnished or unfurnished, Reuben ?"

" That I can't tell you, my lady, but Mr. Hawkins, the agent, at Lymehurst, he told Bob Kent that it was let for a goodish spell, and the gentlefolks would be down most immediately. So I hope they'll prove good customers to Warmouth, for it wants 'em sadly."

" I hope they may," returns Lady Gwynne ; but just at that moment she catches sight of the top of Mr. Barnes' low-crowned clerical hat, rising above the wall that forms the boundary between her garden and the chapel, and leaves her occupation, to run and give him some information respecting the parishioners he has placed beneath her care.

At the same time, a maid-servant steps out of the opened windows of the drawing-room, and advances to the lawn.

"Mamma! there's some one wants to speak to you," shouts Daisy from her garden-chair; but Lady Gwynne is so earnestly discussing the ailments of the old, and the delinquencies of the young, that she does not hear her daughter's summons.

"Mamma is engaged at this moment, Mary," decides Miss Gwynne. "I will tell her as soon as she is at leisure; you can go," and the servant departs accordingly.

In a few minutes Lady Gwynne walks thoughtfully back towards the lawn.

"Mamma, darling! Mary says there's some one waiting to see you."

"Who is it, Daisy?"

"She didn't say; some old woman or other, I suppose. Shall Jack run and ask?"

"No, no, dear! I know who it is. Nelly Barlow come about the Cochin China fowls. But she should have made up her mind before; I have already ordered some from Exeter. Shall I send Miss Ward to you? Emily has not returned from bathing yet; she is very late to-day."

"No, don't send any one; only, come back yourself as soon as you can. And, mother, do tell Nelly I want another kitten. Perhaps she may know of a pretty one."

" Oh, Daisy ! and you have three already."

"Now, mother, you know that Reuben has taken one for a stable cat, and Tommy never comes near the drawing-room, and Bessy is growing up so ugly."

" Well, I suppose it must be so, if my spoilt baby wants it," and the mother's eyes rest with ineffable tenderness upon the prostrate little form before her. Daisy appears to return the affection in full force.

" My own sweet mamma ! I do love you so ;" and she pulls down Lady Gwynne's face to be smothered in kisses, not releasing it until it is crimson with the exertion, and half hidden by her fair tumbled *chevelure*.

" Oh, mamma ! you do look so pretty !"

Lady Gwynne laughs, and shakes back her hair, tucking it away beneath the fastening of her hat, as she walks towards the open drawing-room windows.

She goes straight through them, believing the apartment to be empty, and is startled to find that her entrance causes a gentleman seated at the further end to rise to his feet—still more startled to discover in her unexpected visitor—Auberon Slade!

The shock is great to her, but not so great as it has been in former times, and the only evidence she gives of it, is by sitting down upon the first chair in her way before she has found words wherewith to welcome him; whilst he, apparently more agitated than herself, stands by the table where he has risen, neither coming forward, nor offering his hand.

She is the first to regain her speech and

her composure—why do women always take the initiative in these cases?—and leaving her seat, advances towards him with an outstretched hand.

"How do you do, Mr. Slade? I had not the slightest idea you were here! No one told me of your arrival! How long have you been waiting for me?"

"Oh, not very long," he answers politely, but in a nervous manner. "About ten minutes or so, perhaps."

"So stupid of my servants," she murmurs; "but you must excuse country training." And then, after a pause,— "Are you staying in Warmouth, or only passing through?"

"Well, I may say, I am only passing through. I slept in Exeter last night; but I return to London this evening. You seem to have a charming little place down here—"

"Yes!—it is very comfortable and quiet."

"I thought I might venture, Lady Gwynne, as I was so near, to claim the privilege of an old friend and make you an unceremonious visit. I was so desirous of seeing Daisy again—and—and—yourself, and to learn how you were getting on! You will forgive the unfashionable hour of my call."

"Oh, we are all unfashionable in Warmouth, Mr. Slade, and I am sure Daisy will be charmed to renew her acquaintance with you. She often mentions your name, and has never forgotten your kindness to her. She has grown so much stronger since I brought her here."

"I am very glad to hear it! And will

you think me very bold if I ask you to give me some luncheon ?"

She smiles, but oh ! so sadly, remembering the many meals they have partaken of together.

" I will do so with the greatest pleasure. You, with your Sybaritic tastes, will laugh to hear that we dine at two o'clock ; but you can lunch at the same time. My hours are all regulated by Daisy's. I have no one but her to live for, now——," and then, as though fearing her last words had said too much, she continues, quickly,— "you will meet an old Felton acquaintance also ; Emily Musgrave is staying with me."

" And you like this place,—you find it healthy, and the climate pleasant ?"

" Very much so ! I do not think I ever breathed a purer, or more equable atmosphere."

" And yet you do not look as though it had agreed with you, Lady Gwynne !"

She blushes crimson beneath this remark ; she knows that she has become painfully thin and delicate in appearance of late ; but she is intensely angry that he should be bold enough to notice it.

As for Auberon Slade, he thinks he has never seen so great a change take place in any person in so short a time, and has been regarding her sunken cheeks, and the dark circles that grief has drawn beneath her eyes, with the most painful interest, ever since she entered the apartment.

" Forgive me, Lady Gwynne !—I had no intention of offending you ; but you really do not look well."

" My looks belie my feelings,"—she answers, coldly. " Had you seen the vigour with which I have been gardening all the morning, you would not believe there is much the matter with me. But it is half-past one, and I am really afraid I must leave you, Mr. Slade, to prepare for dinner. Perhaps you would like to make a little preparation for it yourself?"

"I will just brush my hair," he answers sadly.

"Mary will show you to a room," she says, with apparent carelessness, as she rings the drawing-room, bell, and passes from his sight.

But, ushered into the spare bed-room, and provided with all things necessary to his refreshment, Auberon Slade seems far more disposed to resolve into his old trick of falling into a reverie until the second bell shall wake him up again, than to display the activity necessary to the occasion. He leans on the window sill, and watches the old gardener at his work, and the arrival of Emily Musgrave, with her damp hair hanging down her back, and the transport of Daisy from the lawn to the dining-room, and sees and hears nothing of it all, whilst he muses on the altered looks of Gwendoline Gwynne, and dares to guess the reason of them !

Oh ! the torture of a reproachful memory ; the still worse torture of knowing we have done that, we can never again undo ! He thinks, and sighs, and wishes to God he had died months ago, and left her at least the belief he was as worthy as she imagined him to be.

Bah ! what is the use of thinking, or crying over spilt milk ; his fate and hers are fixed—they must make the best of it, as others have to do. But the word "fixed" jogs some lagging memory in his mind, and recalls the jangle of his own verses :

> " Do what we will, thy fate and mine are fixed,
>   My life and thine inevitably mixed."

Pshaw ! What follies our brains do sometimes betray us into, under the influence of cigars and brandy and water ! The Felton mixture must have been a great deal too strong for his head *that* night—there is little doubt of that—And Auberon Slade dashes his face down into the basin of cool spring water that awaits him, as though he were endeavouring to wash away conviction and memory—and the summer dust, at one and the same time.

At the luncheon table he is himself again : and so is Lady Gwynne. He, the polished, gallant, and witty Auberon Slade of olden times, and she, as calm, dignified and graceful in her demeanour, as though she had never known her guest under any other aspect than that in which he now appears. Daisy is naturally clamorous in her welcome, and eager in her demands that "dear Auberon" should come at once and pitch his tent at Warmouth, close to the Orchard House (a contingency, for which her mother heaves a grateful sigh that there is not the shadow of a chance), and Miss Musgrave (who has always entertained a lurking admiration for the fascinating poet) makes herself as agreeable as it is in her power to do; thereby unconsciously, but opportunely, relieving her hostess from the onerous duty of conducting the conversation as though she were enjoying it. And by means of these two talkative tongues is at last produced the result which Lady Gwynne has been longing, yet fearing to bring about—

the introduction of the name of Mrs. Auberon Slade.

" And so you are really married, Mr. Slade !" remarks Miss Musgrave, when they are seated at table. " I was astonished to hear it.   I should never have imagined you had sufficient nerve to make up your mind to such a thing !   And how do you like domestic bliss ?   Confess you are already tired of it, and longing to return to a single life ?" Mr. Slade's mouth at the moment being full of roast chicken and tongue, either the situation or the question, has the effect of making him look very uncomfortable.

" Now, it's no good blushing over it," continues his tormenter, " And particularly as Mrs. Slade is not here to profit by your delicate confusion !   By the way, where *is* Mrs. Slade ? Is she so rash as to have let you out of leading strings already ?"

" She is in London," he replies at last, with an awkwardness that appears comical to all present, except the one who guesses how much pain it carries with it. " We have been staying at her father's, ever since we returned from the Continent."

" Why didn't you bring her with you, Auberon?" interposes Miss Daisy. "Mamma would have been so glad to see her, wouldn't you, mamma?   And I want to see her too. I like pretty people.   And one of your sisters was very kind to me ; she sat nearly a whole afternoon once by my bedside in London, and told me stories about you and Miss Cameron—and she said Miss Cameron was so pretty !"

" My sisters have gone down to Blankshire again," he says, with an evident desire to change the subject.   " I have not seen them since my return ?"

" And when did you return, Mr. Slade ?" demands Miss Musgrave.

" A month ago—I was abroad more than three."

" So much as that ?"

" Why! of course he must have been, Emily. He was married on the 10th of February. I remember that quite well, because it was the very same day that papa ——"

" *Daisy!*" says the soft voice of her mother warningly ; and every one immediately commences to be exceedingly busy with the contents of his or her plate, whilst the spoilt child follows up her *mal-apropos* remark, with the observation that she was sure she didn't know there was any harm in talking about it.

" But all this time we have not heard what business brings you to Warmouth ?"

says Miss Musgrave, with a view to setting the party more at their ease, and Auberon Slade replies in rather a hesitating manner, that he came down to see a friend ; and immediately begins to talk of something else. But, after dinner, finding himself alone in the drawing-room with Lady Gwynne, he speaks more freely.

"You do not seem at all curious to learn what brought me to this part of the country, Lady Gwynne ?"

"I think Emily put the question to you at dinner, and you seemed disinclined to answer it."

"That must have been because I was un-certain how you would receive my news. Will you be glad, I wonder !" coming closer to her, "or sorry, to hear that I contem-plate settling down at Warmouth ?"

The unwelcome intelligence takes her so

completely by surprise that she is thrown off her guard, and the incredulous energy with which she exclaims, " Never !" shows how distasteful the idea is to her. And though the next moment she recovers herself, and follows up her exclamation with the lame excuse, " because it is out of the way; so very far from London !" her first look and word have betrayed her real feelings on the subject, and Auberon Slade answers them alone.

"I did not think—I hoped, at least, that the prospect of our becoming neighbours would have been as agreeable to you, as to myself, Lady Gwynne."

"Oh, of course ! why should it not be ?" though she is trembling all over with agitation. " Only, I scarcely think you can be aware what a very quiet place this is."

"The quieter, the better. The fact

is, my health has been very unequal of late, and the doctors say that if I live in London all the year round, it will break down altogether. Besides mental labour requires mental rest."

"But Warmouth is such a distance from town."

"Only four hours' journey by train."

"It is such a dull place."

"*You* manage to live here."

"Oh, I am different. Daisy takes up all my time. But you—you have a young wife, and I think you ought to consider her. Mrs. Slade has been used to amusement and gaiety, and there is none here."

At this allusion, he frowns.

"My wife must learn to be amused with what amuses me."

"But there is really no society here fit for a young married lady. Besides the doctor's and the clergyman's wives, there is no one living in the place."

" There is yourself, Lady Gwynne."

It is now her turn to frown, and her answer is delivered very coldly.

" I am afraid you must place no dependance upon me, for as I said before, my time is fully occupied, and I visit nowhere."

" Do you mean then utterly to desert me ? Are we never to be friends again ?"

There is an echo of old times in the tone in which he pronounces these words that reaches the very centre of her heart ; and as she answers him, lightly and almost gaily, pulling the flowers about in a vase as she speaks, she is obliged to turn her face away.

" I was not aware that we had ever been anything less. But you must know, Mr.

Slade, that the intimacy of two women who have never seen each other, rests on a contingency. Your wife may not choose to receive me as a friend."

" By Jove ! if she does not."

" Wait a minute—I had not finished my sentence—or I may not take a fancy to her ! You see I am candid with you, but I am so, in order to prevent the fact of my living in Warmouth having any influence upon your choice of a residence."

" Unfortunately you speak too late," he answers gloomily, " I have already signed an agreement to take Fernside."

" For how long ?"

" Three years."

" Oh, I *am* so sorry !"

It is an awkward speech, which slips from her unawares, and is followed by a long silence on either part; he, pulling his moustaches and looking out of the window; and she disarranging all the ornaments upon her drawing-room table.

They are looking to speak the truth to one other—these two, who but so short a time before, shared every thought and feeling—she, to tell him how miserable and unsettled, the prospect of daily meeting him will render her; and he, to ask her pardon for having, by his rash impetuosity, destroyed the little comfort, faith in him had left.

But ah, the bonds and trammels of this world's etiquette—the wretched pride that makes us shrink from confessing we are faithful—it prevents these hearts from speaking for each other's good—it even prompts them to an acted falsehood! She tries to ask him for both their sakes, to relinquish his determination ; even to sacrifice his money, but she dares not ; the very entreaty would betray too much. And feeling that her last speech is indicative of too vivid an interest in his proceedings, she attempts to rectify it by a huge assumption of indifference, and has not rattled about those unfortunate ornaments for more than five minutes before she speaks again.

" What a stupid speech for me to have made ! I *do* feel sorry, of course (at least as sorry as one *can* feel, about a matter of such pure indifference as the taking of a house), but only because I'm afraid you'll be disappointed in your choice. Warmouth is a very stupid place, and full of very stupid people ; so I hope you will prepare Mrs. Slade for what she may expect, beforehand."

" But you will be her friend, will you
not ?"

The question is addressed so seriously
and sadly, that it puts her affected carelessness to flight.

" If you wish it, I will—"

" Thank you—so much !"

Again they both are silent !

The bright June sun is streaming in at
the unclosed windows, the whole place is
hushed and still, everything seems to be
at rest ; except these two turbulent fast-
beating hearts.

" Gwendoline !"

" Yes !" and she turns, and looks at
him.

" Be her friend, be mine," entreatingly.
" She is very young, very ignorant, and
very undisciplined, and God only knows
how it will all turn out ; I don't ; I scarcely

dare to enquire, or to think. But through it all, I have held fast to one hope—that you would stand my friend, and help me."

" Oh! I will, *I will*; I never dreamt of this."

" We won't look back; it is of no use going over old ground, but I am not happy. You may guess so much as that. And I thought—I hoped, perhaps in coming here—"

" I see—I understand it all. You need say no more. And you had my promise— you have it still. I will do what I can to serve you."

She might add, " I will sacrifice myself anew for you—" but she does not.

A true woman never stoops to contemplate the self-denial that she exercises.

" I will not attempt to thank you.

You know better than I could describe, what I am feeling at this present moment."

"Let us go into the garden, it will be cool under the trees ; and you shall tell me all about Fernside.　And I have not shown you my pony and cow yet ; nor my ducks and chickens.　Do come !"

She is all eagerness now to turn the current of his thoughts ; for, with a woman's instinct she sees that they are harking back to the days at Felton, and the dear dangerous moments they passed together there.　Nor is her own mind entirely without need of distraction ; it is as hard for a woman, as for a man, to calmly see the creature she loves, in the possession of another.

And so they talk of eggs, and butter, and cheese, and the profits of a kitchen garden, till the time arrives for her to send him to the nearest railway station in her pony carriage; and she has leisure to believe that it is indeed true ; and Auberon Slade once more about to become her companion and her friend.

The glories of the setting sun have, by this time, long departed from Warmouth, and a dull hazy blue mist settled down upon the valley, and the village.   Yet the eyes of Lady Gwynne, gazing at it from her drawing-room windows, seem able to pierce through the evening gloom, and descry strange figures toiling up and down its hilly paths—and she thinks the little place has never looked so fair to her before.

END OF VOL II.

HILLING, PRINTER, GUILDFORD.